THE BOY NEXT DOOR

G.A. HAUSER

Chapter One

June 28, 1988

"Get in here! Shut the door."

"We're going to get in trouble."

"Shh...just do it quick, before my mom comes up the stairs."

Brandon took one last peek out of the closet they were hiding in. He closed the door, shadowing them in darkness. Zach switched on the small flashlight, illuminated his face from under his jaw, and made a scary *ooh* noise.

Brandon whacked him playfully on the shoulder. "Cut it out. Stop kidding around and let's do it."

Zach tucked the flashlight under his arm and quickly unzipped his pants as Brandon did the same. Brandon could hear their breaths panting at the fear and excitement of doing something taboo.

"Ready?" Zach asked, always the braver of the two.

"Yeah." Brandon bit his lip, looking down. Zach was shining the flashlight on himself.

"See it?"

Brandon nodded. "My turn. Give me the light."

"No, I got it." Zach turned the beam onto Brandon. "What

does it mean when they get hard?"

"I don't know. I was hoping you did." Brandon looked down at himself.

"Shit. I hear a noise!" Zach shut off the flashlight and fastened his pants. In seconds they were stumbling out of the closest, tripping over each other and rushing across the shag carpet to their schoolbooks. Sitting down on the floor, each with a paper in their hands, they listened quietly.

After a minute to calm down, Brandon said, "I don't think your mom is coming up. It sounds like she's still in the kitchen. I can hear her making dinner or something." When he caught Zach's brilliant sky blue eyes, he found that sly look he adored. Instantly, they burst out laughing, rolling back on the floor and holding their bellies.

Wiping his eyes, Brandon finally contained the hilarity long enough to sit up and smile at Zach. When Zach reigned in his laughter as well, Brandon spit on his palm, held out his hand for a shake, boasting, "Best friends."

Zach spit on his hand, gripped Brandon's in a vice-like hold and shook it, confirming, "Bestest friends."

Smiling in pride, Brandon didn't know it at the time, but it was the first spark of love that he was to feel for someone outside of his immediate family. And he never forgot it.

Chapter Two

May 1995

"Brandon! You're going to be late for school."

"Okay, Ma! I'm ready." Brandon scrambled down the stairs, his book bag over his shoulder.

"Zachary is already outside waiting for you."

"Why didn't you say so?" Brandon dashed past her and out the front door. When he stepped outside, Zach's big smile was waiting for him.

"Late again?" Zach grinned knowingly.

Brandon looked over his shoulder where his mother stood at the doorway, watching them go. He waved to her and then said to Zach, "I can't stand waking up in the morning. I wish school was later in the day."

"You're such a dork," Zach laughed. "What are you going to be like in college?"

"I'll make sure all my classes start at ten! Anyway, last baseball practice today, then one more game and we're done," Brandon sighed, looking across the street at a frantic mother and her unruly, screaming toddler.

Glancing at the child's tantrum briefly, Zach asked Brandon, "Were we that bad?"

"No, no way. We were angels," Brandon assured him.

"Anyway." Zach paused at an intersection, "yes, practice today. I love baseball. It's such a cool sport. I'm sorry it's almost over."

As they proceeded across the road, Brandon nudged Zach in the ribs. "You would love it. You're so good at it."

"I know." Zach stuck out his chest proudly, then shouted, "And you suck!" right before he darted away.

Bursting into laughter, Brandon raced after him to the school grounds, yelling in response, "At least I'm smarter than you!"

Dripping with sweat, dirty, and exhausted, Brandon scuffed his cleats to the locker room to shower and change. In front of him, Zach was moving just as slowly. Standing side by side, they peeled off the mud-stained uniforms silently. When Zach was down to his briefs, Brandon peeked over at him. He loved the way Zach's bronze skin shined in the florescent light. He admired his tiny erect nipples and incredibly handsome profile. Zach was the golden boy, the popular class leader and sought after by all the girls. Knowing he was far from ugly himself, Brandon tried not to be envious of his best friend, but he craved all his attention, and sometimes Zach was distracted more than Brandon would have liked.

"Man, I stink," Zach grumbled, taking a sniff under his armpit.

"Let's shower. Come on." Brandon carried a towel with him to the long wall of protruding showerheads. Several boys were already washing under the steaming spray. Trying not to be obvious about his attraction, Brandon set his towel on a hook, stripped off his jockey shorts, forcing himself not to stare at Zach lathering up next to him. Brandon knew if he was caught peeking, or even worse, got excited, he'd never live it down.

The Boy Next Door

"You're coming over after this, right?" Zach asked.

"Most likely." Brandon kept his eyes on the white tile. Behind them the sound of raucous male laughter echoed off the wet walls.

"It's Friday. We can get our homework done and stay up late. Call your mom from my house and tell her you'll be with me."

"Okay." Brandon rinsed and followed Zach out of the shower. He knew if he could, he would follow Zach anywhere.

"Is that you, Zachary?"

"Yes, Mom. Brandon's here. Can he stay for dinner?" Zach dropped his book bag on the floor near the door while Brandon stood waiting for the answer.

"Yes, of course, dear. Hello, Brandon. Do you want me to call your mother for you?"

"Hi, Mrs. Sherman. Okay." Brandon smiled shyly.

"I'll do it right now." Maude picked up the phone.

"Come on," Zach nudged Brandon, "let's get the stupid math homework done. I hate having it hanging over my head all weekend."

Nodding in agreement, Brandon crouched down and dug out the workbook from his bag. In the kitchen he could hear Zach's mom saying, "Lois, it's Maude. Brandon wants to stay for dinner, is that all right with you, dear?"

Brandon knew it would be. His mother and Zach's mother were best friends, as well. Peeking up at the doorway where Maude stood, Brandon received a big smile and wink from her. As the women chatted on the phone about the latest gossip, Brandon sat down at the dining room table with Zach and opened the pages of his book. "Right. Algebra. Oh, these are easy."

"Maybe for you," Zach moaned, rubbing his forehead.

"Which ones don't you get?" Brandon leaned over to look at Zach's book.

"The division of fractions. I swear I can't understand them."

Smiling warmly at the concerned expression on Zach's face, Brandon assured him, "I'll explain it step by step. It's not that hard once you break it down."

"Good. It really stresses me out, Brandy. I hate math."

Glowing with pride at being able to do something good for Zach, Brandon moved his chair closer so they were almost touching, then began explaining the basics of division of fractions.

By six, Mr. Sylvester Sherman had arrived home from work. He loosened his tie as he stepped into the room.

"Hello, Brandon, Zachary. What are you boys up to?"

"Watchin' TV," Zach responded blandly, leaning his chin on his palm on the arm of the sofa.

"Did you do your homework?"

"Yeah. All done."

Brandon wondered when Zach got older if he'd look like his dad. Mr. Sherman was a big, strong, handsome man. Brandon had no doubt Zach would take after him. They had the same muscular build, dark brown hair, and light blue eyes.

"Where's your sister?" Sly asked as Maude came into the room and kissed his cheek.

"In her room," Zach answered, his eyes never leaving the television screen.

Brandon watched the show of affection between Zach's parents and actually felt a pang of jealousy. What would it feel like to kiss? He was seventeen. Wasn't it time to learn that stuff?

"Dinner in five minutes, boys," Maude warned.

The Boy Next Door

"Okay, Mom," Zach answered.

When they had left the room, Brandon leaned over onto Zach's shoulder as they sat together on the sofa. "Your mom and dad really love each other."

"Hmm?" Zach blinked his eyes, as if he hadn't really been paying attention. "What?"

"I mean the way they act. My parents don't, like, kiss or anything. At least not in front of me."

"Ew, gross. Parents kissing." Zach wrinkled up his nose.

"You ever wonder what it would be like to kiss someone?" Brandon stared directly at Zach's soft lips.

Zach shrugged. "I suppose."

"Shandy Ellis is always drooling over you in class."

Zach's stoic expression cracked a smile.

Brandon felt slightly let down Zach was amused by the information.

When Sly returned to the den, he had an envelope in his hand. "Here, Zach. I have a feeling this is another acceptance letter. Now you have several choices where to go. But this is the college I was thinking about. Have you made up your mind as to which one you're going to go to?"

Brandon sat up, moving away from Zach. Zach took the paperwork from his father, pulling the letter and brochures out of the packet. Sly sat down across from them. "Lower the television volume, would you, Brandon?"

Brandon found the remote control and shut off the set completely.

"Yes, you're right, Dad. It's an acceptance letter from NYU."

"Yes. Listen, Zachary, just because you're already accepted to a few different schools doesn't mean I don't expect you to get good grades on your finals."

"You know which school you want to go to?" Brandon

asked in amazement. As far as he was concerned that decision was too overwhelming to make. He had several different colleges to choose from as well but had always hoped they would go to the same one.

"Sort of." Zach peeked up at his father's stern expression.

Answering for him, Sly said, "I want him to get into engineering, like me."

"Oh." Brandon nodded, but got the feeling his best friend wasn't interested in that line of work.

"Dinner!" Maude announced.

"Come on. Wash up, boys." Sly stood.

Zach set the brochures down on the coffee table. Brandon followed him to the closest bathroom. Once they had their hands under the tap of running water, Brandon asked, "You don't want to study engineering, do you?"

"No. No way. It's too much fucking math."

Brandon shook off his hands and then dried them on a towel. "What do you want to do?"

"My Uncle David is a lawyer. He told me I should study law. But, I still have to get my bachelor's degree in something. Just not in engineering. It's too hard a major."

Trailing behind Zach, out of the bathroom and into the kitchen with its fantastic scent of roast chicken and potatoes, Brandon whispered, "Is your dad going to mind?"

"How could he mind having his son a lawyer?" Zach scoffed. "I'll just get my undergraduate degree at NYU and go on from there."

Nodding , Brandon wondered if it was time for him to think of a career as well. Though he'd been accepted to three different schools, he still wasn't completely sure of a major. He thought he had time to decide. But this was May of their senior year and the idea of Zachary going to one college and him going to a different one was enough to bring him to tears.

The Boy Next Door

Zach's little sister Hannah sat down at the table next to him. She smiled at him adoringly.

"Hello, Brandon..." she sang flirtatiously.

Glancing at the thirteen-year-old girl shyly, Brandon said hello back, then caught Maude's kind smile.

By ten o'clock Brandon was completely exhausted and struggling to keep his eyes open. "I should be getting home." He stretched his back, getting up off the couch.

Zach perked up, having been off in a dream world. "Okay." He stood to escort Brandon to the door.

"Goodnight, Mr. Sherman, Mrs. Sherman." Brandon waved to them. They had all been watching television together in the den.

"Goodnight, Brandon," they replied, smiling.

Once he and Zach were standing alone by the front door, Brandon picked up his book bag and leaned on the doorframe. "See ya tomorrow for the last baseball game?"

"Yeah. I'm going to try and sleep late. I really feel tired."

"It's from the extra practice after school." Brandon wondered what Zach would do if he leaned over to kiss him.

"Probably. Okay, Brandy, see ya tomorrow."

Nodding, knowing he'd never have the nerve to try, Brandon left Zach behind, walking next door to his own home. When he looked back, he noticed Zach still there and waved to him. He got a wave back. Brandon hated when they parted. He always felt like he was in solitary confinement.

The door was unlocked. Brandon stepped in and listened for noise. He put his books down and found his parents in the den watching the TV.

"Hello, son," Mel said softly.

"Hi, Dad." Brandon sat down next to him on the soft velour sofa.

"You have a nice dinner at Maude's?" Lois had knitting needles on her lap and a beige mass of yarn had begun to take the shape of a rectangle.

"Yeah. She made some chicken. It was good." Brandon paused a moment. "I have to decide which college to go to now, don't I?"

"Yes, Brandon, it's time," Mel replied, lowering the sound on the television.

Lois set down her knitting and asked, "Reece is going to Princeton, Brandon. You did get accepted there. Is that where you want to go?"

Thinking about his older brother, knowing they didn't get along very well, Brandon shook his head. "How about NYU? I was accepted there as well."

"NYU?" Mel asked. "Why NYU? Did you just pick that out of the three, or do they have some kind of program you'd be interested in?"

Lois interjected before Brandon answered, "What do you want to do for a job, Brandon?"

Sitting back, Brandon knew that would inevitably be the question. What did he want to do? Could he follow Zach's lead? Become a lawyer? He had no desire to debate, to argue. No.

"Brandon?" Mel asked.

"Uh…I'm not sure. Do I have to decide now?"

"Yes, in a way you do. You can start off by taking some mandatory courses, but you do have to have an idea what you will major in. Don't you at least have a clue?" Mel prodded, a slight sound of frustration to his voice.

Brandon sighed, "Right. I have to decide."

"What's brought all this on? I thought you had a good idea what to study. Didn't you mention journalism?" Lois asked.

"Well, Zach is planning his career in law."

His parents exchanged knowing glances. Brandon felt

slightly embarrassed by it. He knew it seemed as if he couldn't live without that adorable boy next door.

"Don't worry about it, Brandon. It will work out." Lois touched Brandon's arm gently.

"Right. Goodnight, Mom, Dad." Brandon stood up, kissed his mother on the cheek, then headed to bed.

Washed and changed into his pajama bottoms, Brandon climbed into his snug bed and sighed. If only he could tell Zach what he really thought. But that option scared him to death.

Clark, the skinny redheaded boy in class, was teased mercilessly about being gay. No one really knew if Clark was gay, but it didn't seem to matter. He was slight, shy, freckled, and fair game to the bullies in the class. Odds were Clark wasn't even remotely interested in boys. Regardless, the teasing was merciless. Though he'd never heard Zachary say a disparaging word about poor Clark, Brandon did watch Zach when they witnessed the carnage. Always the same expression appeared on Zach's face; a slightly upturned curl to one side of his lip. It was unreadable to Brandon. Was it amusement or disdain? Brandon couldn't begin to guess. He only knew that revealing his sexuality now, at seventeen, would bring him more agony than it was worth. He had time. Later. Maybe when they were in college, maybe they would be roommates. Maybe...maybe...

Growing tired, Brandon finally shut his eyes and fell asleep.

Chapter Three

Spring was working its way to summer as the temperature rose to almost eighty degrees. Brandon tossed the ball to Zach who was wearing his Fair Lawn High baseball uniform and a cap to shield the glaring sun. The team was ready for their last game of the year before graduation. Some of the boys were running sprints, some batting, others catching and pitching.

It amazed Brandon how muscular Zach's body was becoming. Like Zach's father, Zachary was growing big and powerful. Even his arms were showing that incredible masculine definition of biceps and deltoids that most young men had to work out in a gym for hours to achieve. Brandon knew if he kept becoming mesmerized by Zach's body, he'd soon have a hard-on to deal with.

Brandon waved to his and Zach's parents who were in the stands to watch them play.

Finally, the umpire flipped the coin to see who was up first. Brandon and Zach rooted for each other to get that big hit out of the park each time they were up at bat.

Brandon could hear Zach's father screaming, his voice getting hoarse from his highly competitive nature. Zach appeared to be ignoring him, rolling his eyes at Brandon as if the man were embarrassing him with his uncapped enthusiasm.

After three hours of whacking the ball and running bases, Zach and Brandon approached the stands where they were congratulated by their family. Sly patted Zach's back so hard, Brandon thought he'd break him in two.

"We'll see you guys at home, okay?" Zach said to his parents. They nodded, waving, and walked out of the stands with Brandon's parents following closely behind them.

Once they were on their own, Brandon and Zach headed to the locker room, sweat dripping from their faces and necks. All the boys were high-fiving each other at the win, and congratulations rang out loudly in the bad acoustics.

"We should just head home and swim in my pool." Zach wiped his forehead with the back of his arm and took off his cleats.

"Has your dad got it all set up?" Brandon began to unbutton his hot uniform shirt.

"Yeah. He said he would have it done today. Wanna check?"

"Skip a shower?" Brandon stopped mid-strip.

"I don't care. We could jog home, then change when we get there."

Wondering if he had that much energy left, Brandon caught that competitive glimmer in Zach's eye and couldn't resist. "You said jog, right? Not race?" Brandon changed his cleats for his sneakers.

Closing his locker with a bang, his running shoes on his feet, Zach started walking backwards to the exit, a wicked grin on his face.

"Oh, come on, Zach! We just played for hours." Before he could shout out another word, Zach had already sprinted out of the locker room.

Re-buttoning his shirt as he raced after Zach, Brandon cracked up with laughter even though he was completely spent. Seeing Zach skipping, twisting around, as if giving him a chance to catch up, Brandon pumped his weary legs and tried his best.

The mile walk home was now a mile run. Brandon struggled not to drop dead from the heat and exhaustion as an invigorated Zachary seemed to be dancing in glee.

Finally tripping towards the front porch of Zach's house, Brandon deliberately dropped down on the soft green lawn, gasping for breath. Spread out on his back, looking up through a maple tree at the shimmering sunlight, Brandon held his chest and recuperated. A shadow covered his face. There, smiling adoringly at him, was the ever-charming Zachary Emerson Sherman. "You suck," Brandon teased.

Zachary shook his head quickly from side to side, spraying sweat droplets on Brandon as he lay prone.

"Ew!" Brandon sat up "Stop! That's gross."

Zachary collapsed on the cool shady grass next to him. Looking over at Zach, Brandon found him also catching his breath and staring up at the fresh lime-green foliage. Rolling to his side, Brandon tugged a grass shoot from the lawn and chewed it, staring at him. "Three more weeks, then graduation."

"I can't wait." Zach faced Brandon, leaning his head on his palm, mirroring Brandon's posture.

"You going to get a job this summer?" Brandon watched a tiny perspiration drop roll down Zach's temple to his high cheekbone.

"Most likely. Dad pretty much insists on it."

"At Memorial Pool again?"

"Probably."

"As a lifeguard?" Brandon struggled with the urge to brush that drop of sweat off Zach's face.

"Yeah. Easy money." Zach pulled out a blade of grass to gnaw on. "I don't want to work in dad's office. I did it once, hated it."

"I remember."

"What will you do?"

"I don't know. My parents aren't that pushy. They don't force me to work if I don't want to."

"It's good to have the extra cash. I'm saving for a car."

A wash of chills made its way over Brandon's hot skin. Zach had so many plans made already it scared him. Brandon didn't want to be left behind.

"Right." Zach sat up, spitting the grass out of his mouth. "I'll meet you in the backyard."

"Okay." Brandon made his way to his feet and headed to his front door. When he entered the house, the cool air-conditioning caressed his overheated skin.

"Brandon?"

"I'm home, Mom," he shouted back.

"Okay, honey," she acknowledged, "Great game. You are my star! How are you feeling? Tired?"

"Hot! I'm going over to Zach's for a swim to cool off."

She approached him, coming into the living room just as Brandon was about to climb the stairs to his room. "Oh? His father has the pool ready? It's early this year."

Brandon shrugged. "Zach said he was getting it done."

"I suppose it's a good thing. It's very hot out." She looked over Brandon's dirty baseball uniform. "You need to get that into the wash."

"I will."

"You want lunch first?"

"I was going to just change into my swimming suit and head over."

"I'll make some sandwiches you can take."

"Okay." Brandon took the stairs two by two. Entering his room, he dug through his drawers for his swimsuit. It was last year's, but he hoped it still fit. Stripping off his clothing, Brandon tried on his old pair of black Speedos and found them very snug. When he looked into the mirror he could see the outline of his penis clearly. "Oh, shit! I can't wear these." Moving to the top of the stairs, Brandon yelled, "Ma!"

"What?" came the distant response.

"My bathing suit is too small! I think I must have grown since last year."

"What?" Lois hurried to the bottom of the stairs.

"My bathing suit is too tight." Brandon gestured down at it.

"Is it? It looks like it fits you okay."

"Mom, no way!"

"I don't know what you want me to do about it now. Do you want to go shopping?"

Looking down at himself, he knew if he got even a slight erection it would be impossible to hide it. Brandon rubbed his face in irritation.

"You want me to see what your father has?"

"Can you?"

"Give me a minute."

When she disappeared from the bottom of the stairs, Brandon walked back to his room and looked in the full-length mirror. The trunks were low on his pelvis and high on the thighs. If Zachary wore something similar, Brandon would be so excited by it, he'd have to hide. Sticking his hand down the front, he tried to position his cock so it didn't show as much. It was useless.

Brandon jumped when his mother rapped her knuckles on his door. Not wanting to be caught touching himself, he asked her to come in when he was ready.

"Here are your father's swimsuits." She held out two gaudy, floral-printed old man trunks.

"Oh, no way. What about Reece? Did he leave anything behind?"

"I don't know what's wrong with the ones you're wearing,

Brandon. They fit you fine."

Feeling self-conscious, Brandon covered his hand over his crotch and mumbled, "I feel naked."

"Don't be silly. You're just not used to being in a swimsuit after three months of winter." She left the room, then shouted, "Besides, honey, it's just you and Zachary. I don't know what you have to be so self-conscious about."

Hearing her descend the staircase, Brandon looked back into the mirror echoing in his head, "It's just you and Zachary…"

Sighing, Brandon slipped a pair of shorts over the tiny suit. When he was ready he jogged down the stairs. Lois handed him a bag of sandwiches and a beach towel. "Don't get too sunburned. You want some suntan lotion?"

"Okay." Brandon waited as she rushed to find it. Tossing the towel around his neck, Brandon took the bottle from her and then left through the front of the house, walking around the small low shrubbery to the fence along the side of Zach's house. He opened the latch and pushed back the gate.

"What took you so long?" Zach shouted, already submerged in the pool.

"Sorry." Brandon shut the gate behind him and set his towel down on a lounge chair. "My mom made sandwiches." He held up the bag.

"Cool. My mom's making something, too."

Zach swam to the ladder at the deep end of his built-in pool and climbed out. When Brandon realized Zachary's swimsuit was as tiny as his own, he didn't know whether he felt relieved or petrified.

Tearing his vision away from Zach's crotch, Brandon set the food down on a table with an umbrella shading it, then opened the bag as Zach sat down next to him.

"What are they?" Zach reached out his hand.

Investigating one before he gave it to Zach, Brandon

replied, "Turkey and cheese?"

"Cool." Zach devoured the food like a starved prisoner.

"Is your dad or sister joining us?" Brandon chewed his sandwich.

"No. Dad took Hannah to the mall. Mom's inside."

"Oh." *Good.* "So, we have the pool to ourselves?"

"Yup."

Seeing Zach had already stuffed the whole sandwich in his mouth and swallowed, Brandon hurried to do the same.

Maude stepped out onto the patio with a pitcher of lemonade. "Hello, Brandon."

"Hi, Mrs. Sherman."

"My, it is hot out. You two better put some sun-block on."

Brandon showed her the bottle he brought. "Mom gave me this."

"Well, use it. It's very warm out today."

"We will, Mom." Zach rolled his eyes at Brandon.

"Oh, you have sandwiches. Do you want more?"

"No, we're good." Zach poured two glasses of lemonade.

"Okay, boys. I'll be inside. Just call if you need me."

"We won't." Zach laughed.

After Maude disappeared, Zach stood up. "Come on. Let's get in the water."

"Aren't you supposed to wait a half hour after you eat?" Brandon was already erect just staring at Zach's amazing chest and biceps.

"That's such crap. You sound like a dork." Zach jumped into the pool.

Taking a last sip of the lemonade as if it were a shot of booze for courage, Brandon stepped out of his shorts and glanced down at himself. *Yup, a hard-on.*

As quickly as he could, Brandon plunged into the pool,

feeling more at ease concealed under the water.

Zach watched Brandon carefully. Getting a glimpse of him in his tiny swim trunks, he licked his lips unconsciously and wondered just how much privacy they had before his mother stepped outside again or his father and sister came home and joined them.

Brandon swam over to Zach. Zach was in the deep end, holding onto the aquamarine colored edge of the pool by the diving board. Dunking under, Brandon slicked back his long hair and then wiped the water from his eyes. "Feels great. I wish we had a pool."

"You don't need one. You can use ours."

"I know. Thanks. Wouldn't it be cool to sneak out at night and take a dip?"

"Skinny dip!"

The wild look in Zach's eyes made Brandon chuckle. "Skinny dip? Are you kidding? In your parents' pool?"

"Yeah! We could come out at like midnight when they're asleep."

Brandon blinked at him curiously. He and Zach? Naked? Alone in the pool? Was that even remotely possible?

Zach stared into Brandon's brown eyes. What was he thinking? Did Brandon think he was nuts? Or? Could he be tempted?

They were together since the day they were born. Zach remembered the stories his and Brandon's mother told about their being pregnant at the same time, how their births were only a month apart; Brandon born August third and Zachary born July third. The women would giggle and explain to them that since the day Brandon and he could walk the two of them were inseparable. Was that why he and Brandon were so close? Or was it something else? As their eighteenth birthdays drew nearer, Zach's urges became more urgent. He just couldn't decide if it was because he felt safe with Brandon, comfortable, or if he truly preferred men. Zach had no clue and certainly couldn't talk to anyone about it.

Brandon began to salivate as he stared into Zach's light blue eyes. The reflections from the water made his irises appear almost turquoise. The fantasies he was spinning in his head were overwhelming him. The two of them? Naked? Alone?

"Let's do it. Tonight," Brandon hissed.

"Really?"

"Yes!"

"Cool!" Zach grinned wickedly.

"I bet I can even sneak out some booze."

"Even cooler!" Zach quieted down, and looked back at the sliding doors of the back of his house.

"Midnight?" Brandon asked in excitement.

"Midnight." They spit on their palms and shook on it.

After some horsing around in the pool, the boys climbed out and sat down on the lounge chairs. Brandon sipped the lemonade from the sweating glass and sucked it down to the bottom thirstily.

Clearing his throat, Zach whispered shyly, "Ah, you want me to put some of this stuff on you? You know, so you don't burn?"

Choking on the last sip, Brandon's eyes grew wide and he nodded.

Zach took a quick glimpse at the back of the house, just to see if anyone was watching, then he squirted a blob of lotion in his hands and rubbed them together. Holding up two cream-covered hands, Zach asked innocently, "Where should I start?"

"Uh..." Brandon glanced down between his legs first. "My back?"

"Okay. Turn around." Zach waited as Brandon moved so his back was facing him, then Zach began rubbing the thick cream over Brandon's hot skin.

Knowing what would happen, Brandon kept staring at himself and could see the outline of his erection through his tight Speedos. Though he was mortified by it, the sensation of Zach touching him was worth any amount of anxiety he was feeling. As his head fell forward limply, Brandon closed his eyes to savor the caressing. Never, *never*, had Zach touched him like that before.

After a pause and the sound of the plastic tube spitting out more goo, Brandon felt those strong hands reaching over his shoulder and down his chest. Zach's hands were moving in circles over Brandon's nipples and down the front of his stomach. It was too much. Brandon jumped as Zach's fingers brushed the top of his bathing suit.

When Brandon moved out of his reach, Zach surfaced from the trance he had fallen under. Hypnotized by the feel of Brandon's body under his slippery hands, Zach couldn't believe the sensation of fire it sent to his crotch. In his mind he had imagined he would coat every inch of Brandon's tight hard body, slide his hands down Brandon's thighs, his arms. But when Brandon jerked away, Zach felt crushed.

Panting, trying to slow his breathing, Brandon met Zach's light eyes. What was this about? Did he mean it? Was he just coating him with cream or was it something more?

The sound of the sliding door opening scared them both. Brandon grabbed his towel and covered his lap quickly.

"Well!" Sly announced. "Here are my two champion ball players! I'm so glad to see you both out here enjoying the pool. You mind if Hannah and I join you?"

Brandon crossed his legs and adjusted the towel on his lap as Zach replied in a calm clear voice, "No. It's okay, Dad."

"Great!" Sly disappeared back inside the house.

The minute he did, Brandon stood up and jumped into the pool. As the cold water calmed his body down, he twisted around to see Zach putting the cap back on the bottle and wiping his hands off on a towel.

Brandon wondered if they would still meet for their midnight swim. His head was so light from the touch of Zach's hands he felt dizzy.

In a few minutes Sly and Hannah had joined them. Splashing, dunking and throwing a beach ball around, Brandon had to wait until nighttime for his answer.

He couldn't sleep. Staring with wide eyes at the clock, begging for the time to move by in hours instead of minutes, Brandon was becoming a nervous wreck. At eleven-thirty he climbed out of bed and put on his damp bathing suit, slipping a pair of shorts over it and a t-shirt. Tiptoeing down the stairs, listening for any sound of movement, he grabbed a bottle of beer from the refrigerator and left through the back door. He walked around to the side gate at Zach's house. Unlatching it, he opened it slowly, closed it, and when his eyes focused he found a silhouette in the moonlight. Zach was already reclining on one of the lounge chairs. Hurrying over to him, Brandon whispered, "I thought I was too early. How long have you been out here?"

"Only a half hour. I couldn't sleep."

Brandon placed the beer bottle down on the table, taking a seat next to him. "Me neither."

"Here." Zach handed him an open bottle of wine.

Brandon took it, gulping it down hastily from his nerves.

"I've already got a mean head-buzz."

"Okay. Let me catch up." Brandon took another gulp as Zach twisted open the beer and started on that as well.

After a few quiet moments, they swapped bottles.

Brandon finished the beer, wiped his mouth with the back of his hand, then stood up boldly and pulled the t-shirt over his head.

Like it was a dare, Zach rose up, unsteady on his feet, and removed his shirt.

Crickets, night birds, dogs barking in the distance surrounded them in a misty surreal dream. The pool was lit by underwater lights giving it an illuminating glow as if it were phosphorescent.

Brandon slipped off his shorts, pausing, his thumbs in the waistband of his bathing suit, waiting for Zach to catch up. Staring at each other, Brandon heard Zach counting to three. On the last number, they both dragged their clothing to their ankles.

Feeling his stomach flipping nervously at the idea of being caught naked together, Brandon kicked off the small swimsuit at his feet and covered his crotch instinctively.

"When you get in, don't make a splash," Zach whispered, slurring his words.

Brandon nodded, following him to the ladder, staring at his tight round ass as it seemed to glow in the dim light. Slowly, they eased into the pool, breast-stroking their way to the deep end. Once they were in a spot by the wall, they hung on side by side.

"This is so cool." Zach's white teeth gleamed from his tanned face.

"I've never done anything like this before."

"Oh yes, we have." Zach laughed quietly.

"When? When the hell did we skinny-dip together?"

"Not skinny-dipping. But we did something like this before."

Brandon struggled to figure out when.

Finally, Zach moved closer, their legs brushing under the cool water. In Brandon's ear he breathed, "Remember when we were ten? In my closet, upstairs in my room?"

Instantly, Brandon did. "Oh...that."

"Yeah...that," Zach echoed. "I asked you if you knew why it got hard."

Chuckling to himself, Brandon nodded. "We were such dorks." Zach gripped Brandon's hand under the water. Brandon's eyes sprang wide open when he felt Zach leading it to his body. The minute Brandon felt Zach's hard-on, he thought he would die inside.

"It's hard again."

"You...you...?" Brandon wanted to ask him something to clarify this act. Was this just as innocent as it was seven years ago? Just some experiment? Or was it something more.

"I what?" Zach inched closer, their legs began to interlock as they hovered in the water.

Brandon wanted to release the arm that was keeping him attached to the side of the pool, but they were in deep water and would sink. Before he could ask another question, Zach moved his left hand behind Brandon's head and drew him to his lips.

At the first touch of Zach's mouth, Brandon began sucking on the alcohol taste left by the beer and wine. The zinging sensation through his belly when their tongues touched was making him swoon. Parting from that hot mouth reluctantly, Brandon whispered, "Move to where we can stand."

Even though it was closer to the back of the house, Zach nodded and tread water backwards until their feet felt the firm bottom. The minute Brandon could stand, he wrapped his arms around Zach's neck and attached to Zach's mouth again. Under the refreshing water, Brandon felt Zach's cock, hard, pointing straight out, rubbing against his own. And that kiss. Never had Brandon imagined what a kiss would be like. You could see it a thousand times on television and in the movies, but until you kiss someone yourself, you can't imagine the thrill. They couldn't get enough of mashing their lips and tongues together. Brandon could hear Zach's heavy panting as he, too, couldn't seem to get enough air. A hand grasped Brandon's dick. Surprised by the act, Brandon jerked his hips back in reflex, then relaxed as he felt Zachary's hand moving the way Brandon had done to himself. Zach knew. Zach knew exactly how to do it.

Needing more oxygen before he passed out, Brandon parted from Zach's mouth. He spread his legs wide as Zach's hand worked him feverishly causing the water to ripple and splash gently. Unable to stop it, Brandon felt his body erupt with orgasmic chills. "I'm...I'm..." Brandon wanted to warn Zach, but Zach whispered, "Come...spurt...come..." Zach urged, moving his hand even faster.

A cloud of misty sperm ejaculated out of Brandon's body. In the dim night lights of the pool it swirled around their hips and thighs like smoke.

"Do me...do me..." Zach found both of Brandon's hands under the water and attached them to his cock.

Still spinning from his first non-self-induced climax, Brandon was gulping the air and his knees felt weak. With two hands he gripped Zach's cock and instantly felt Zach pumping, thrusting into them. Trying to get his brain to stop feeling woozy and pay attention to what he was doing, Brandon opened his eyes and found a look on Zachary's face that he couldn't quite believe.

His head thrown back, his eyes sealed shut, Zach's teeth were barred in the most lustful expression Brandon had ever seen. He held Zach's cock tighter, jerking it off like he meant it. As he ogled that incredible boy's face lit by moonlight and the pool's ambient glow, Brandon watched the climax wash over

Zachary. A burst of hot liquid hit Brandon's hip, then quickly dispersed. Still holding tight to that pulsing cock, Brandon gazed at Zach's eyes, waiting for them to open. When they did, Brandon felt like bursting he was so happy. Wrapping around each other, they once again met mouths, sucking and licking at each other's tongues and teeth. They didn't say anything. What was there to say?

Brandon never imagined touching someone could bring so much physical and emotional pleasure. And the relief that Zachary shared in the attraction was so overwhelming, he imagined from then on life would be bliss. He could die now. He had tasted Eden.

By two a.m. Brandon crept back to bed. Dreading the noise of a shower waking everyone up, he used a washcloth to get the chlorine off his body, then crawled under his sheets. He was so sated sexually and so satisfied mentally, he drifted off the minute his head hit the pillow.

And next door, exactly the same scenario was played out, until two very exhausted boys were deep in slumber.

Chapter Four

Waking, seeing it was nearing ten in the morning, Brandon hopped out of bed and raced to his window to look out at Zach's house. From his bedroom he could see a glimpse of the corner of the pool and the windows to the east side of the house. Dashing to the bathroom to wash up, Brandon splashed his face and brushed his teeth, staring at his reflection, trying to decide if last night was some incredible dream or if—just if—he could have been naked in that pool with Zachary Sherman.

Racing out of the bathroom, jumping into a pair of shorts, Brandon needed to verify it was not a dream. Jogging down the stairs, seeing his mother on the phone, Brandon raced outside and sprinted next door. Catching his breath after ringing the doorbell, he pushed his hair back from his face and waited. Crossing his arms over his chest, he leaned back to look at the house, trying to see inside, then rang the bell again. Wondering if the doorbell was broken, Brandon knocked. No one answered. "What the?" He sat down on their porch and tried to remember if Zach had mentioned if he was busy or not.

Finally, hearing his mother shouting for him, Brandon walked down the two steps and headed to where she stood, holding the front door open for him.

"Why did you race out like that? Don't you want breakfast? I've made some waffles." As Brandon entered the house, she added, "Your father has already eaten his. I've got some warming in the oven for you."

"Okay." Brandon sat down at the table, running his hand through his hair as he tried to think.

Lois set a glass of orange juice down on the table for him, then began fixing him a plate with waffles and bacon. "No one home next door?"

"No. I can't remember where Zach said he had to go."

"None of your other friends are around?" She set the plate down and then a bottle of maple syrup.

"I don't know." Brandon began devouring his food hungrily.

His mother joined him at the table, sipping a cup of coffee. When she reached out and brushed his hair back from his forehead, he met her eyes. She was smiling sweetly at him.

"You okay?" he asked, chewing and swallowing quickly.

"My little boy is almost grown up," she mused, misty-eyed. "Soon both my boys will be in college."

"I'll probably commute. I won't go to Princeton like Reece did." He stuffed a slice of bacon into his mouth.

"That would be nice. I'm not ready for you both to be gone."

Swallowing some juice first, clearing his throat, Brandon asked meekly, "Mom, how old were you when you had your first boyfriend?"

Seeing her slight surprise at the question, Lois softened her expression and thought about it. "I suppose I was around your age. Sixteen, seventeen. A boy asked me to the senior prom. Why? Is there a girl at school you're thinking of asking to the prom?"

Brandon became mute. In a million years he couldn't imagine telling his mother he liked boys.

Smiling, she stood up and took Brandon's empty plate to the sink. "Well, I suppose it is about time for you to have those feelings, Brandon. Do you want me to ask your father to talk to you about…you know… being with a girl?"

"No!" Brandon held up his hand. "No…I'm all right on that."

Facing him, her hands on her hips, Lois admonished, "Are you sure? I don't want you in trouble. You know what I mean. Making a girl pregnant…"

"Mom…" Brandon moaned.

"We had a close call with your brother. I'm warning you, Brandon, we don't want to go through that again."

"Don't worry. Okay, Mom?" Brandon stood up and headed to the front door.

"Where are you off to?"

"I don't know. Just for a walk."

"Okay. See you later, honey."

Brandon waved, heading out into the warm sunshine.

Zachary sat in his grandmother's living room, bored out of his mind. Checking his watch over and over, he wondered how he got roped into a day wasting his time at Granny's. A large lunch was in the oven. All he wanted was a sandwich and a soda and then to go home!

Hearing the rest of the family in the kitchen, Zachary stood up and leaned into the room. "Grandma, can I use your phone?"

"Sure, dear," she replied.

"Who do you have to call?" Sly asked.

"Just Brandon."

Nodding, Sly continued to chat with his wife and mother.

Finding an extension in his grandmother's bedroom, Zach sat down on her frilly bed and dialed, inhaling the smell of floral scented soap that seemed to permeate the house. "Hello, Mrs. Townsend? It's Zach. Is Brandon there?"

"Oh, Zachary. He just went out for a walk. He checked your house earlier and didn't find you home."

"I'm at my grandma's," he moaned. "Can you tell him I called? And that I'll be home around three?"

"I will."

"Thanks." Zachary began to twiddle his thumbs, staring at his lap. "I'm going nuts without you." Zach peeked back at the open door and noticed Hannah staring at him. "What are you doing there, ya pest? Listening in on my call?"

"I'm bored."

Sighing, Zach stood up and met her at the door. "Me too. When can we leave?"

"Dad said not until after we eat."

"Shit."

"Ooh! You swore." She pointed, covering her mouth.

"Shut up."

As she raced back to the kitchen, Zach could hear Hannah shouting, "Zachary swore!"

Shaking his head in frustration, all Zach wanted was to be with Brandon. He wanted to ask Brandon what he thought about last night. Would he do it again? Or was it just one crazy drunk night?

Instinctively, Brandon walked towards the high school. Before he made it to the campus grounds, he stopped at a park with a swing, slide, and metal stagecoach to climb on. Sitting on one of the cool steel bars of the red painted coach, Brandon leaned over his lap and tried to get his thoughts organized. The future was looming. Which college did he want to go to and what would his major be? What kind of car should he get? It was as if time had caved in on him and his long unfettered youth was slowly merging with his adulthood choices. He wasn't ready. He wanted to go backwards and stay aloof, uncommitted to a decision he wasn't ready to make. What did he want to be when he grew up? Well, it seemed growing up was only months away.

A cold chill passed over his back even though the temperature was already climbing as it neared midday.

At the sound of voices, Brandon sat up and looked around. A group of high school students approached. Standing, wondering if he should move on before they instigated something, Brandon was about to get going when someone actually called his name.

"Townsend!"

Slightly relieved to see the captain of the baseball team, Brandon stuffed his hands into his shorts' pockets and walked to the crowd of half a dozen boys. "Hey, Truman."

"What are you doing out here by yourself?"

Looking behind Truman, seeing several smirks ready to shout sarcastic comments, Brandon mumbled, "Just thinking."

"Where's your Siamese twin?" one sneered, then guffawed in a loud hyena laugh.

Brandon knew whom he meant. Was it that obvious that he and Zach were connected at the hip?

Truman shouted to the rude boy, "Shut up, Baxter, you asshole."

Not wanting to hear another comment, Brandon nodded to Truman, "See ya."

"See ya," Truman replied.

As Brandon walked past the group, he endured the staring eyes. About to snap, "What the hell are you looking at?" but decided against it. The odds weren't stacked in his favor. Feeling more isolated and confused than usual, Brandon scuffed his worn out sneakers towards home.

Zach felt as if he were finally cut off the leash. Before he even changed out of his good clothing, he jumped out of the car and raced to Brandon's door. When Lois answered, Zach asked, "Is Brandon in?"

"Yes. He's been waiting for you. He's up in his room. Come in." Lois leaned out the front door to wave at Zach's parents as they loitered outside.

Zach raced up the stairs quickly and stood at Brandon's bedroom door. Listening first, Zach debated whether he should knock or just barge in. Smiling wickedly, he swung opened the door. Brandon had been sleeping on top of the bedspread. At the noise he jumped and sat up. Zach grinned in excitement and closed the door behind him, then leapt on top of him on the bed.

"What are you doing? My mom and dad are home!"

"Did you like it? Last night? Did you think about it?" Zach squirmed all over Brandon's warm body.

Brandon's face softened with an affectionate smile. "I can't stop thinking about it."

"Me neither." Zach leaned up on his elbows and looked at the door.

As if reading his mind, Brandon whispered, "Not here. No way."

"Come on...just a little." Zach yanked the shirt tail out of Brandon's shorts and stuffed his hand down the front.

Brandon stiffened his back, his eyes never leaving the door. "I'll be dead! I swear!"

"I just love the way you feel," Zach groaned, gripping Brandon's cock in his fist. Biting his lip in concentration, Zach worked on Brandon's dick in the tight space of the inside of his shorts. "Spurt, spurt…" Zach encouraged quietly.

With shaking hands, Brandon moved his shirt higher on his chest, opening his zipper. "Don't get it on my clothes."

"'K'." Zach sat up and got a better grip. Licking his lips, he stared from Brandon's face to his crotch and back again. Zach heard Brandon inhale sharply. A spatter of white creamy liquid shot out onto his chest. "Do me, do me…" Zach yanked down the zipper of his good slacks and got to his knees.

Brandon was panting in hard puffs, looking back at the closed door every few seconds.

Holding his cotton shirt up, Zach arched his back, sticking out his hips as Brandon jerked him off. Having been thinking of nothing else all day, Zach came quickly.

Brandon gasped and tried to contain the spray. "Shit!"

Zach opened his eyes and found Brandon cupping his sperm in two hands. He roared with laughter as Brandon looked around in panic for something to wipe it off with.

When they heard Brandon's name being shouted from downstairs, they jumped off the bed and straightened up their clothing. Brandon cleaned his hands and stomach on a dirty sock and then checked back with Zach before opening the door. Zach nodded.

Brandon stepped out to the hall. "Yeah?"

"Zachary's parents want us to come over for dinner."

"Okay," Brandon answered.

"It'll be late, around seven, is that okay with you guys?"

"Yeah," Brandon yelled down the stairs. When nothing returned in reply, Brandon shut his door again and looked back at Zach.

Smiling wickedly, Zach opened his arms, his palms facing forward, yearning for Brandon's embrace.

Brandon fell against him, wrapping around him tightly. Then to Zach's pleasure, Brandon whispered, "I never felt anything like it, Zach."

"Me neither. I'm addicted to your hands. I can't stop thinking about it."

"It feels so much better when you do it. I mean, I do it to myself, but it feels different when you do it. Does that make sense?"

Chuckling softly, Zach replied, "Yes. Believe me, I understand."

"Can I kiss you again?"

"Yes!" Zach crushed Brandon in his embrace. Opening his lips he accepted Brandon's tongue, immediately growing hard again at the meeting of their mouths.

Brandon loved the way Zach's tongue felt against his own as it swirled it sent shivers to his crotch. Standing in the middle of his bedroom, making out with this adorable hunk, Brandon was living a dream. All his fears suddenly faded, and he felt as if he could do anything with Zach by his side.

Chapter Five

On Monday morning Brandon tried to feel motivated for school and his final exams. Unfortunately, he only could think of one thing. Zachary Sherman. His book bag on his shoulder, he met Zach out in front of his house and they walked the mile to the high school. "I'm ready for graduation. I am so tired of school."

"Man, you complain a lot." Zach shook his head, smiling at him.

"What? Are you telling me you like it?"

"No. But it doesn't do any good to whine."

"Sorry." Moving closer so their shoulders where brushing, Brandon whispered, "I'd just rather be naked with you all day."

"Stop that. I don't need a hard-on for homeroom."

"When can we do it again?" Brandon looked around the street. Several other students were making their way to the various learning establishments.

Zach shrugged. "After class?"

"Good. I can't wait."

Shandy Ellis crossed the street when they came close to the entrance of the school. "Hi, Zachary. Brandon."

"Hey, Shandy," Zach greeted her.

"You guys going to the prom?" She batted her lashes in

Zach's direction.

"Prom?" Brandon asked. "Why would I want to go to the prom?"

"Because it's romantic!" She waved at some girlfriends excitedly. "You have to get tickets now. Before it's too late."

Brandon rolled his eyes tiredly at Zach. "Who needs a stupid prom?"

When Zach didn't answer, Shandy nestled closer to him, whispering, "I'd go with you, Zach, if you needed a date."

Brandon bristled, glaring at her. Zach met his eyes and shrugged as if he couldn't help it if he was irresistible. "Come on, Zach. We'll be late for homeroom." Brandon nudged him.

"See ya, Shandy." Zach waved at her. "Hey, wait up," Zach grumbled to Brandon as he caught up to him inside the school. "What's with you?"

Brandon couldn't wipe the pout off his face. "I don't like her flirting with you."

Grabbing Brandon's arm, Zach stopped him and took him aside in the crowded hall. Through a tight mouth, Zach whispered, "Look, if you think I want people thinking I'm queer, you can forget it."

"So?" Brandon challenged.

"So, I'm going to talk, flirt, and even possibly take a girl to the prom."

"What?" Brandon felt crushed.

"Just for the look of it, you dork!" Zach peered around the hall quickly. "And if you don't want rumors flying about you, you better consider it, as well."

"I'm not dating a stupid girl."

"That's your choice, Brandy, but don't blame me if they start treating you like Clark."

As Zach said the boy's name, Brandon spotted the slight redhead trying to appear invisible as he walked down the hall.

Once that warning was spoken, Zach mumbled, "See ya later," and left.

Brandon felt sick to his stomach at having to hide his sexuality or, worse, pretend he liked girls. And the thought of Zach having a date with one made him so jealous he could scream. Grinding his jaw as he went, Brandon made his way to homeroom before the bell sounded.

At lunch Zach spotted Brandon sitting by himself in the cafeteria. Loading up his tray with the daily special, Zach headed over to sit with him, nodding his head to greet several other classmates as he passed. Resting his tray down in front of him, Zach realized Brandon must be in a world of his own because Brandon didn't look up when he sat down across the table from him. "What's going on?"

Brandon slowly raised his head, meeting Zach's eyes.

Waiting for a comment, Zach stared into those brown orbs and could tell Brandon was still stewing over the morning discussion. Seeing Brandon wasn't talking at the moment, Zach began eating his food, watching Brandon intently as he did.

The sound of some loud tormenting made its way through the noisy room. Zach raised his head to see the usual suspects making fun of Clark again. Shaking his head sadly, Zach continued eating until suddenly Brandon began shouting at the bully, "Hey! Leave Clark alone!"

"What the fuck are you doing?" Zach whispered in fury.

Ignoring him, Brandon yelled across the room, "Pick on someone your own size, Baxter!"

"Brandon!" Zach snarled.

"What's it got to do with you?" Baxter roared back.

Zach couldn't believe his ears. Why the hell was Brandon risking his neck for Clark? Zach put down his fork so he could focus on the insane battle. Baxter was standing at their table, looming like a big lummox. Brandon had stood up, puffing out his chest in anger.

Waiting, Zach pushed his tray aside and watched the contest in anguish.

"You got a problem, Townsend?" Baxter spat.

"Yeah! You, you fucking asshole. Why don't you just lay off the kid?"

"I'll do what I want! And if you don't like it, lump it!"

"What the fuck did Clark ever do to you, you fat freak?"

Zach rubbed his face in agony as the fight escalated. Meanwhile, Clark and a dozen other students were watching the debate in awe.

Baxter grabbed Brandon's shirt collar. Zach was about to stand up and separate them when suddenly Baxter went flying backwards from one of Brandon's right hooks.

A gasp went up from the spectators. Then someone yelled, "Vice principal! Vice Principal Bowman is coming!"

Immediately, the crowd went about its business. Baxter crawled to his feet, trying to hide his red swollen face. A warning glance from the wounded boy made its way back to Brandon before Baxter disappeared into the crowd. In the noise of the bad acoustics, everyone continued to act normal. Brandon sat down, wriggling his right hand, shaking off the pain of the punch.

Zach waited for Brandon to meet his eyes. Prowling down the aisles of the cafeteria as if he smelled blood, the vice principal eyed each student suspiciously.

Once he passed, Zach hissed, "Nice one, Brandy."

"I'm sick of them taunting Clark. For cryin' out loud, the kid can't defend himself."

"Hell of a punch, babe." Zach grinned at him.

Finally breaking his stone-like expression, Brandon began laughing.

Zach leaned over the table. "I think Baxter may lay off for

a while now. You foxy heavyweight champ."

"Either that, or he'll get five other guys to jump me."

"Don't worry about it. You can handle them." The minute Brandon caught his eye, Zach winked affectionately.

After school they walked together in the muggy heat back to their neighborhood. Brandon's knuckles felt sore, and he was surprised how much they hurt. When Zach noticed him moving his hand, he grabbed it and snuck a kiss to Brandon's knuckles. Brandon looked around and said, "That was brave of you."

Zach shrugged. "I was amazed how you decked Baxter. I didn't know you had it in you."

Grinning wryly, Brandon replied, "Maybe there's more to me than you think."

"There is. I know!"

"Your house or mine?" Brandon asked.

"How about mine? After we do our homework, we can swim."

"Okay." Brandon smiled happily.

As they came through the door, Zach shouted to see if anyone was home. No one replied. "Good. Mom's most likely gone to pick up Hannah."

"Cool. You want to get a snack first?"

"Okay." They set down their books and hunted in the refrigerator for food. Once they had devoured some leftovers, they headed up the stairs to Zach's bedroom to sit on the floor and get their work done.

Brandon stretched out on the carpet, his textbook in front of him as he propped himself up to read the chapter. Beside him, Zach was sprawled out on his back, the book hovering over his face. The dry information making its way into his brain cells, Brandon scribbled some notes and highlighted a line here and there.

Zach yawned "Done reading?"

"Yeah. Where are the practice questions we had to answer for the final?"

"Page two hundred and ten."

"Right." Brandon stretched his back and then read the first one out loud. "Oh, I found that answer… It's in my notes."

Within a half hour they had finished the assignment. Brandon rolled to his back and said, "I was going to read ahead, just to get a jump on studying."

"Okay." Zach lay next to him.

"Want me to read it out loud?"

"Sure."

Holding the book over his face, Brandon began reading the next chapter. As the bland facts left his mouth, he felt Zach move so he was connected to his side, then Zach slid his right hand down the front of Brandon's shorts. It seemed the contact was merely meant to relax them both and not stir them into a frenzy of excitement. Brandon continued reading, enjoying the gentle massage of his pubic hair, cock, and balls. When he glanced over at Zach, Zach's eyes were closed and his face was passive as if he too was just glad to be touching Brandon's private parts, knowing he had exclusive rights to them.

Nearing the end of the chapter, Brandon imagined closing the book, setting it down on the carpet, and rolling over to kiss Zach's lips. Suddenly, he heard a tiny sound of an inhaled breath. It caught both of their attention.

Brandon lowered the book and found Hannah standing at the bedroom door with her eyes as wide as two ping-pong balls. Zach jerked his hand from out of the front of Brandon's shorts. Before Brandon's brain could comprehend, Zach was on his feet, racing after her, calling Hannah's name.

His heart in his throat, Brandon set the book down on the carpet and tried to catch his breath.

The Boy Next Door

"Hannah! Hannah, get back here!" Zach gripped her elbow and stopped her progress to the stairs, and inevitably to the kitchen where their mother was. He dragged Hannah into her pink frilly bedroom and closed the door. "What did you see?" he asked her.

"I'm telling!"

"Hannah!" Zach shook her to make her pay attention. "We weren't doing anything!"

"Yes you were!"

"No! You're wrong! We were just doing homework. You got that?" Zach shook her again.

"Why did you have your hand down Brandon's pants?" she whispered, her face appearing like a parody of shock.

"I didn't! So don't go telling Mom lies."

"But I saw you!"

"Hannah!" He gripped her tightly, making her look into his face as he crouched down to her level. "You remember when you broke Mom's favorite vase? Remember?" She nodded fearfully. "I didn't rat on you. Did I? Did I tell her I knew you broke it?" She shook her head. "I didn't. I pretended you didn't do it because I knew how mad she would get. Now, listen to me, Hannah..." He made sure she was paying attention. "I'll deny you saw anything. I'll tell Mom and Dad you were lying. And," he growled, "I'll tell them you broke Mom's vase when you were pretending to be a ballerina in the living room. You understand, Hannah?"

She nodded, her eyes never losing the appearance of fear.

"And don't ever just barge into my room again. You know better than that. You knock first. You hear me?"

Another frightened nod followed.

"Now. I want your promise."

"I promise."

"You promise to what?" Zach pushed her to say something

more.

"To not tell Mom that you were touching Brandon's—"

"Hannah!"

"I promise, Zach."

He was about to release her when she asked again, "But, why were you touching him there?"

Brandon was a nervous wreck. Visions of their lewd conduct being revealed and both sets of parents lecturing them on not being gay, forbidding them to see each other, or worse, grounding them for life, were going through his head. After what felt like an hour, Zach returned, looking very stressed out. Brandon sat up, waiting.

"I made her promise."

"Shit. She's such a little tattletale. Can you trust her?" Brandon stood up.

"What choice do I have?" Zach ran his hand back through his thick dark hair.

"I can't believe she saw us." Brandon had butterflies in his stomach.

"We better get out of this room. Let's go sit by the pool or something."

"Okay." Brandon collected his books and put them back into his bag, carrying it down the stairs behind Zach. Before they left through the back of the house, Brandon set the bag by the front door. He boldly faced Maude who was busy making dinner in the kitchen.

"Hello, boys. Done with your studying? Exams are coming!"

"Yeah," Zach answered. "We were going to sit outside."

"Going for a swim?"

"Maybe later." Zach opened the sliding door.

"Are you staying for dinner, Brandon?" Maude asked

sweetly.

"No, thank you, Mrs. Sherman. I probably should go home."

"Okay, dear."

Following Zach, Brandon caught Hannah staring at him. Giving her a bitter frown out of reflex, Brandon headed out into the sunlight and dropped down on a lounge chair.

The rest of the afternoon they were both quiet, trying to have faith in a very immature thirteen year old.

Chapter Six

Every time Brandon realized his mother was on the phone with Zach's mom, he shivered in fear that Hannah had opened her mouth. But, as the weeks moved on and nothing happened to indicate Hannah had broken her promise, Brandon began to relax and have faith in human beings again.

Wonderful mid-May, nearing the last days of their senior year, had finally arrived and final exams were just a memory. The buzz in the hallways about the senior prom was like a swarm of insects. Brandon felt completely enraged when Zach bought tickets and asked the shyest girl in the senior class, Audrey Flannagan, to go. Enduring Shandy's snarls of jealousy, Zach kept pestering Brandon to buy a damn ticket so no one would think he was gay.

"It's bad enough you're so pretty, Brandon. And after what you did for Clark in the lunchroom..." Zach shook his head.

"What do I care? I'll never see these idiots again. We'll be in college next September, Zach."

"I'm going. I don't need my father asking me questions about it. He's been on my ass every day trying to see who I was taking to that stupid dance."

"Why? What does your dad care, Zach?"

"Oh, he cares, Brandy. You have no idea how much." Zach leaned against his locker and relaxed.

The Boy Next Door

The last few days of class felt like an exercise in futility. With the exams done, hardly any of the seniors were even showing up, and all the teachers did was sit around in groups discussing everyone's future aspirations.

"Just a few more hurdles, Brandy. Prom, graduation, then summer job, then college. We're almost there."

Seeing the dreamy expression on Zach's face, Brandon grumbled, "Stupid prom."

"Come with me! We'll ditch the girls and go get drunk."

"Yeah?" Brandon wondered if that was possible. "Who should I ask?"

"I don't know. Don't you like anyone?"

"No. Not really."

"What about Reagan Banner?"

"Reagan?"

"Yeah. No one will ask her. She seems pretty nice. Sporty, you know."

"I always thought she was a lesbian."

"Perfect!"

Brandon shook his head in disbelief as the bell rang signaling that they needed to go to class.

With the time running short, Brandon spotted Reagan talking to some other female classmates and knew she would think it was completely bizarre for him to ask her to the stupid dance. But she was the best candidate for a girl who wouldn't want to be kissed at the end. Tapping her shoulder, Brandon smiled as she spun around. "Ah, can you spare a second?"

"Sure, Brandon." She waved to her friends and walked down the hall a few paces with him.

"I know it's last minute, and I'm sorry about that, but are you already going to the prom with someone?"

She seemed completely stunned.

Brandon sighed, "Never mind."

"No. No, I haven't been asked. I just can't believe you aren't going with someone like Alyssa or something."

"Alyssa?" Brandon turned up his nose. "No thanks!"

"Yes. I'd love to go with you. Thanks, Brandon."

"Oh, cool. Uh, I suppose we could meet here, or if I can get someone to give us a ride…"

"I'll give you my home number." She wrote it down on a paper and handed it to him.

"I'll let you know," he said, waved to her and hunted for Zach. *Fine! There! A stupid date for the stupid prom!*

Next on the agenda was the purchase of two tickets. He located the table where a gaggle of cheerleaders were schmoozing with the football players and nudged his way to the front. "Two tickets to the prom, please." Brandon took out his wallet.

"Going with Alyssa?" one crooned as she tore two tickets off the roll.

"No… Thanks." Brandon took the tickets and left, not looking back. Under his breath he muttered, "What the hell is with all this Alyssa crap?"

Chapter Seven

Dressed in a tuxedo with a choking bow tie, Brandon posed for the camera while his mother and father gushed over him. When the doorbell rang, he raced to it and found Zach in the same monkey suit.

"My dad's driving us to pick up the girls." Zach whispered, "Got a bottle of blackberry brandy in my sock."

"Thank fuck. I need a drink. What a waste of time."

"Shut up and keep smiling." Zach waved goodbye to Brandon's teary-eyed mom who kept repeating that her little baby was all grown up.

Sly sat behind the wheel, beaming proudly at them both, as if this night confirmed their leap into manhood, or some other heterosexual ritual that Brandon could hardly stomach. Listening to Sly's boring stories of his own experience with a girl at the prom, Brandon tried not to gag at the gory details.

First they stopped for a photo opportunity at Audrey's house, then the same ritual at Reagan's, until Brandon was so tired and frustrated with the charade he could scream.

Dropped off at the school's main entrance, they walked through halls, which were covered in balloons and streamers as the worst hits of 1995 made their way down from where the DJ spun the discs.

After an obligatory first dance with the girls, Brandon

nudged Zach to get them all some punch and finally speak to him alone. When they were standing over the pink liquid, Brandon moaned, "This sucks! I don't want to be here, I don't want to dance with her, and I want to go somewhere and cop a feel of your cock!"

"Shh!" Zach looked around in paranoia, secretly tipping the booze into two of the cups, tucking the flask into his waistband. "Here. This one's the booze. Give Reagan the straight one."

"How long do we have to stay?"

"I don't know. A few hours I guess." Zach sipped the alcoholic mixture and flinched at its potency. "After a few of these, Brandy, you won't give a shit. Come on, they're waiting."

Shandy Ellis body-slammed Zach as he walked across the dance floor. She was waltzing with Baxter at the time. In a snide voice she said, "Oh, excuse me, Zachary. I didn't see you there."

"Yeah, whatever." Zach shook his head and tried to contain the spill of one of the drinks.

"Hey, Zach," Baxter greeted him and shot Brandon a nasty glare, remembering the punch to the jaw.

"Hey," Zach replied, then nodded to Brandon to keep moving.

"What a bitch," Brandon whispered, looking back over his shoulder at Shandy's scowl.

"Forget her. Look, be nice to Reagan, she's a decent girl."

"I'm not doing anything!"

Two hours later, drunk and weary from the boring dance, the heterosexual act, and the yammering conversation, Brandon checked his watch and asked Zach, "When's your dad coming?"

"I have to call him."

"Call him. Please. I'm dying."

Checking on Audrey and Reagan first, seeing them giggling and smiling happily together, Zach nodded and left to find a payphone.

"Thank fuck!" Brandon groaned in relief.

"One more dance?" Reagan asked sweetly.

"Sure." Brandon tried to be polite. The minute they went onto the dance floor, the music changed to a slow song. Reagan moved close, wrapping her hands around Brandon's neck.

After some rhythmic swaying movement and no conversation, Reagan said, "Thanks for asking me, Brandon."

"No problem. Thanks for coming."

"I know we're not going to date or anything, but it was nice to just be able to go."

"Yeah, I suppose."

"Are you ready for college?"

"Yes. How about you?"

"Definitely!" She sighed. "I can't stand high school."

"Well, at least we have something in common, Reagan."

They danced quietly, then, to Brandon's shock, Reagan whispered, "I like girls."

At the admission, Brandon leaned back to see into her face. She bit her lip, as if waiting for the nasty reply. But Brandon simply smiled back at her. "I know. I think it's cool, Reagan."

"You know? And you asked me to the dance anyway?"

"Yes."

She gaped at him. "Do you like boys?"

Looking around in acute paranoia, he figured since she had shared her secret, he would share his. "Yes."

"Zachary?"

"No. Zach doesn't like guys." He wasn't going to ruin Zach's reputation.

"Oh, too bad. I thought you two made a cute couple."

Holding her close, feeling her chin rest on his shoulder, Brandon looked for Zach in the crowd. He was dancing with Audrey. When their eyes met, he and Zach smiled warmly at each other. *Oh, yes, we do make a cute couple.*

Chapter Eight

As the temperature climbed into the eighties and nineties, Brandon craved dunking in a pool more and more. Except this time, he didn't head next door. Getting on his ten-speed bike, a towel tied to his seat, Brandon rode the long straight line of Berdan Avenue to that large swimming hole in the ground, Memorial Pool. Coasting down the slight hill, the junior high school with the same name came into view along with the white sandy beach surrounding the large man-made lake. Brandon slowed down as he jumped a curb and rolled across the paved walkway to the fenced area around the food pavilion. Hopping off his bike, chaining it to the metal fence, Brandon kicked off his sneakers to walk on the hot sand with bare feet. The area was already packed with locals enjoying the heat wave, sitting under umbrellas or splashing in the water. At the deep end of the lake, three diving boards stood out in front of the first aid building. The highest had the biggest line of waiting daredevils.

Spotting whom he had come to see, Brandon grinned in delight, dropped his towel and sneakers on an open spot near the diving boards, where all the cool high school kids hung out, and stripped down to his bathing suit quickly. Strutting towards a lifeguard, his Memorial Pool badge pinned to his hip, he was no longer paranoid of his body in the skimpy outfit. Brandon stood next to one of the high metal chairs where a Greek god of a young man sat, his baseball cap on his head, and a whistle around his neck. Craning his head up, shielding the glare from

G.A. Hauser

the sun behind them, Brandon shouted up, "Help! I'm drowning!"

Zach peered down at him calmly. "Hey, Brandy."

"When do you get off? Or get a break?"

Zach checked the big clock on the first aid building. "I'm done at one. Can you wait fifteen minutes? Or will you die without me?"

Pretending to choke, Brandon gasped, "I'll die…"

Distracted by some action in the pool, Zach blew his whistle and shouted for two people to stop horsing around.

Brandon smiled at him proudly, boasting in a quiet voice, "I do love it when you're forceful."

Zach peered around the area. "Shut up."

Chuckling to himself, Brandon said, "I'll be waiting."

"Okay."

A big grin plastered on his face, Brandon walked back to his towel, spreading it out neatly to recline on it. Inhaling deeply, he took in the view of the entire area. As usual, girls lingered around the handsome lifeguard, but Brandon didn't let it bother him anymore. He knew Zach was completely committed to their relationship. Over seventeen years they had shared every secret with each other, and for the last two months, they had shared their bodies. If it was a case of trust, Brandon knew he had Zach's. That was enough.

As promised, fifteen minutes later, another young man with a whistle strung around his neck made a move to climb up on the high chair. Brandon sat up as Zach climbed down, chatting for a minute with the persistent Shandy Ellis and one of her tittering friends. Finally, Zach made his way over.

Brandon looked beyond Zach to the two girls. They were watching, whispering to each other. Once he was in Zach's shadow, Brandon glanced up at him.

Zach was staring down at Brandon's body boldly.

"Hey, sailor, come here often?" Brandon teased.

After glancing around quickly as if checking who was within hearing range, Zach whispered seductively, "I love you in that thing."

"This?" Brandon gestured to his swimsuit.

"Yes. I can see your dick right through it." Zach looked around again in paranoia.

Feeling a surge to that area as they spoke, Brandon was sure any moment Zach would know he was excited.

"I have to check out." Zach pointed to the first aid house. "Give them back their whistle."

"Okay." Brandon sat up, wrapping his arms around his knees to hide his erection.

"You hungry? Want to get something at the refreshment stand?"

"Sure."

"I'll be right back."

Nodding, Brandon watched Zach's confident stride as he headed into the shady hut. The amount he loved Zach amazed him.

A second later, Brandon was startled by Shandy and Alyssa jumping heavily on the sand next to him. "Hi, Brandon," Alyssa sang dreamily, crouching down.

"Hi. What do you guys want?"

"Shandy and I want to know if you and Zach want to come to a make-out party tonight at Zelene's house. Her parents are going out of town and she's having a party."

Adding as an incentive, Shandy said, "Everyone will be there."

"A make-out party? Who's supposed to be making out?" Brandon laughed in amusement.

"Well…" Alyssa leaned closer. "I want to make-out with you, Brandon."

As she batted her long lashes, hoping to entice, Brandon tried not to cringe. Behind her, Zach was returning from the first aid hut.

Once Zach stood over the three of them, a beach towel around his neck, he asked, "What's up?"

Speaking as fast as humanly possible, Shandy caught Zach up on the news of Zelene's party. Brandon watched Zach's face for his response. When Zach shrugged, as if to say they "might" come, Brandon shook his head frantically in panic.

"Cool!" Shandy grabbed Alyssa's hand. "See ya there!" The two girls giggled their way back to the group of friends they were sitting with.

Brandon stood up, slipped his shorts on and grabbed his towel. "Why the hell did you give them the idea we were interested?"

Zach watched Brandon step into his sneakers. "I told you. It's all about image. Don't you get that?"

"Yeah, yeah..." Brandon grumbled and walked with Zach to the refreshment stand to get some food.

Once they had eaten burgers and fries, Brandon belched and then stretched his back tiredly. "I could use a nap."

"Where did you park your bike?" Zach asked.

"Over there." Brandon pointed.

"I'd say we could go back to my place, but I know my parents are there. Dad took a few days off to catch up on some projects around the house that Mom's been bugging him about." Zach took off his ball cap and rubbed his head

"How about going up there?" Brandon pointed to an area of trees and grass behind the parking lot.

"Okay." Zach put his cap back on his head and threw out the trash from their table. Carrying their towels, they made their way into the stand of tall trees. Under the canopy of leaves the air felt cooler and more tolerable. In the foreground, picnic tables were set up for families who brought baskets of food with them. Beyond the main picnic area, the shrubs grew higher and more concealing. Under a swaying birch tree, Brandon spread out his towel. Zach did the same, so they were side by side. Exhausted by the muggy heat, they dropped down and groaned tiredly. Brandon kicked off his sneakers and brushed the dry sand from his feet, emptying the grains from the inside of his shoes. When he looked over at Zachary, he was laying on his back, the ball cap pulled down, covering his eyes. Smiling at him, Brandon rolled to his stomach and rested his head on his arms, then instantly fell asleep.

Zach woke. Pushing the cap back from his forehead, he looked around the area and found it isolated. Having no idea what time it was or how long they had napped, he stared down at Brandon as he slept. Zach pretended to brush some grains of sand from off Brandon's tanned naked back but eventually ended up caressing Brandon's warm, smooth skin lovingly.

Feeling Brandon stir under his hand, Zach smiled to himself. Was there anyone else in this world he adored more than Brandon?

Waiting for him to come around, Zach touched Brandon's long brown hair. "Hey."

"Hey," Brandon replied, clearing his throat. "What time is it?"

"No idea. I don't have a watch."

"How long did we sleep?"

Zach laughed, "I don't know the answer to that either."

As if he could tell the hour just by looking around, Brandon sat up stiffly and took in their surroundings. "It must be close to dinner time because no one's up here anymore."

"I guess." Zach smoothed his hand up Brandon's thigh.

Brandon peered down at it. "Uh…we're outside, Zach."

"I know where we are, Brandy."

"But, I mean, people could walk by."

Zach made a deliberate scan of the area. "You see any people?"

Standing up to get a better view, Brandon took his time investigating that answer. Finally, he said, "No."

Zach tugged Brandon to sit back down. Slowly, Brandon did. "What are you planning on doing? Out here...in public?"

Amused by Brandon's nervousness, Zach shrugged. "What do you want to do?"

"Uh? Here?"

"Yup. Here." Zach smoothed his hand over Brandon's crotch.

"Are you kidding? What if Shandy or Alyssa or one of her stupid friends is spying on us?"

"They're not. They most likely all went home for dinner." Zach popped open the button of Brandon's shorts.

"How can you be sure?"

"Brandon, calm down. If we go home we can't go near each other. What are we supposed to do?"

Brandon exhaled. "You're right."

"I know." Zach pushed Brandon's shorts down revealing his bathing suit. He reached into those tight Speedos, exposing Brandon's tan line and hard cock.

Brandon began panting in anxiety, looking around at the quiet trees.

Loving the feel of Brandon's penis, Zach worked it with his right hand, then stuffed his left hand between Brandon's legs to be able to stroke his balls. Licking his lips, wanting to feel it pulsate, Zach hissed, "Stop worrying and come, will ya?"

After an uneasy breath, Brandon lay back, closing his eyes.

"That's it...man, you get so hard..." Zach increased his speed, then by accident one of his fingers touched Brandon's anus. About to apologize for it, Zach heard Brandon breathe in urgency, "Do that again!"

"What? Do what again?" Zach felt his heart beat faster. "What? Do what, Brandy?"

"Touch my ass...touch my ass!"

"Are you kidding me?" Zach hissed in amazement but immediately pushed his finger near it. Instantly, Brandon arched his back and came, grunting in pleasure.

As Brandon recovered, using his towel to clean up, Zach gaped at him. "Was it good? Was it good?"

"Holy shit..." Brandon blinked in astonishment.

"Touching your ass? It felt good?"

"Holy shit..." was all Brandon could manage to say.

Scrambling to get his shorts down his thighs, Zach lay back on the towel and ordered, "Do it to me! Brandon! Do it to me!"

Getting his bathing suit up and fastening his shorts first, Brandon moved to sit next to him. After another look around, he held Zach's cock in one hand and dug between his thighs with the other.

Zach tried to spread his legs with his shorts halfway down, waiting for something good. He was so hard from watching Brandon come, he knew it would take nothing to make him climax. "Ah!" Zach choked.

"What?" Brandon panicked and stopped.

"No! Don't stop! Push in! Push in!" Zach urged, feeling that timid finger enter him gently. The surge to his loins was so intense, Zach had to bite his lip not to shout out loud. The electricity of the contact was like something had clicked a switch to a charge of dynamite. Clenching his jaw on his loud vocalization of euphoria, Zach shut his eyes tight and shot come up into the air.

"Holy shit!" Brandon backed up in order to not get covered in it.

Taking a very long moment to internalize the connection between his ass and his cock, Zach caught his breath.

"See! I told ya!" Brandon pointed at him. "What the fuck? I don't get it. Did it make it like twice as good or what?"

Still stunned by the sensation of chills running over his skin, Zach couldn't put into words what he was thinking. It was such an unexpected connection he was confused by it.

Thinking he heard something, Brandon tried to cover Zach's body up. "Pull up your shorts, Zach," Brandon whispered.

Forcing himself to move, Zach wiped off the semen with his towel, then yanked his bathing suit up and buttoned his shorts. Standing, straightening his cap, he did see someone picking up trash nearby. "Let's go." Zach shook out his towel and then draped it around his neck. With Brandon beside him, Zach walked back out to the beach. A few people lingered in and out of the water. Moving so they could see the time on the clock, Brandon whispered, "Shit. It's almost five."

"Wait." Zach held him back before they headed to their bicycles. "Brandy..."

"Yeah?" Brandon whispered.

"I...we have to do that again...I mean...I want to figure out what happened to make it feel like that."

"I know. Too bad there's no one we can ask."

"I don't need to ask someone. I just wish we had a place that was private where we could experiment more."

"Wow," Brandon said. "And, like, do what?"

"I don't know. All we do is jerk each other off. You know? And I'm not saying that's not great. But if we can do stuff that feels like that..." Zach pointed back to the woods, "shit... I mean, wouldn't you want to get an orgasm that intense all the time?"

"I have no idea where we can do it."

"I do." Zach grinned demonically.

"How late are you going to be, Brandon?" Lois asked as she followed him to the front door.

"I don't know. No later than midnight."

"Whose house is it again?"

"Zelene's. Don't worry, Mom. Her parents are there. It's just for her close friends to celebrate graduating. There won't be any booze or anything."

"You have the phone number to Zelene's house?"

"Ma!" Brandon whined. "I'm seventeen years old! I'll be getting my driver's license this month. Give me a break."

"Is Zachary going with you?"

"Yes. Of course."

"Okay. You guys just stick together and watch out for each other."

Smiling, trying not to gloat, Brandon replied, "You know we will. See ya later." He waved to his mother, heading over to Zach's front porch. As he approached, it seemed as if Maude was going through the same routine argument with Zach.

"Don't worry, Mom...I will!" Zach shouted as he left the house.

"Hey." Brandon smiled wickedly at him.

"Hi, Brandy."

"Everything okay?"

"Yeah, just the usual third degree from my parents." Looking down the street, Zach asked, "Ready?"

"Yup."

"She lives on Orchard Street, right?"

"Yes, that's what I heard."

"Okay."

Making their way to Fair Lawn Avenue, the boys walked

briskly towards the party.

As they drew near, it became obvious which house had no parental control. A keg of beer was already on the front porch hidden by a towel, the spout sticking up like a fishing pole.

As they entered the chaos inside, Brandon nodded in greeting to the few friends he knew and looked around in awe at how out of control the party already was. And it was only eight o'clock.

Shandy and Alyssa waved to them in excitement from across the room. Brandon rolled his eyes in irritation as Zach smiled politely.

"Have a beer." Zach handed a small paper cup with some frothing ale in it to Brandon.

Brandon took it and chugged it down in one gulp. Wiping his mouth with the back of his hand, he said, "More please."

Laughing, Zach poured more and handed it back to him. "Right. Let me stake out the place."

"Cool," Brandon whispered. "What should I do?"

"Nothing. Wait here."

Nodding, Brandon watched as Zach disappeared into the crowd. Fidgeting in excitement, Brandon downed the second beer as quickly as the first, then was trapped into a conversation with some nerdy boy who wanted to be the next Bill Gates.

After two more tiny cups of beer and what felt like an eternity, Zach returned. "Got it."

"Good." Brandon shifted from one leg to the other.

"What are you doing?"

"Have to piss."

"This way." Zach tilted his head discreetly.

Brandon followed him up the staircase, trying to be invisible. Pausing at the top landing, the hallway dark from no windows or lights, Brandon bit his lip on another comment and waited. Listening, Zach finally moved in a direction, opening a door.

When Brandon peered in, he realized it was the master bedroom. Feeling very nervous they would get caught, Brandon was about to abort the plan when Zach latched the door from the inside.

"There's a bathroom through that door."

Brandon opened a door to a closet.

"No, that one." Zach shook his head and redirected him.

Brandon found the right room and was very glad to relieve himself. After he urinated, Brandon washed his hands and checked out his face in the mirror. "Man, are you drunk," he whispered to his reflection.

Opening the door, peeking out, he gulped audibly to find Zach naked, seated on the master bed. "What are you doing?"

"Shh! Get undressed and get over here!"

With trembling hands, Brandon stripped, dropping his clothing in a small pile by the foot of the bed. As he climbed onto the mattress, he asked, "You sure the door's locked?"

"Yes. Now get over here."

Brandon moved closer.

"Lie on your back and spread your legs."

Obeying the orders as if he were a soldier, Brandon did as he was told. His chest rising and falling rapidly from nerves, he craned his neck off the pillows to see what Zach was up to.

"Tell me if what I do is good or bad, okay?" Zach sat between Brandon's bent knees.

Nodding, holding his breath from the suspense, Brandon waited. Zach stroked his testicles. "Good...good..." he whispered. Next Zach wet his index finger by stuffing it into his mouth. "What are you...?" When that wet finger got shoved into his ass, Brandon gasped, "Good! Good!"

"Shh!" Zach hissed. "Okay. How about this?"

That wet digit began to move in and out. Brandon thought

he would pass out from the pleasure. Opening his lips, his hips rising in falling in reflex, afraid he would shout, he waited for Zach to ask how it was.

"That feels good?" Zach asked again.

"Holy shit! But get something to coat your finger with. Not just spit."

Zach jumped off the bed and disappeared into the bathroom. He emerged holding a jar of petroleum jelly. Getting back into position, Zach coated his finger and began where he had left off.

Brandon closed his eyes. "If you touch my dick I'll spurt."

Sitting back, Zach moved to kneel more closely between Brandon's thighs. Curious about what he would do next, Brandon watched Zach through his straddled legs.

Using the jelly, Zach got busy again, only this time Brandon couldn't see what he was doing. Something pushed into his ass. Closing his eyes, Brandon felt a wash of pleasure cover his skin like lightning. "Whoa…" Brandon peeked at Zach. Zach's eyes had closed, and he was pumping his hips feverishly against Brandon's bottom. "Zach? That's not your finger, is it?"

"Ah! Ah!"

"Zach?" Brandon watched in absolute amazement as Zach seemed to spontaneously combust. "Zach?"

Choking from the intensity, Zach backed up and gasped, "You gotta try this…oh, holy shit."

"What? Try what? What did you do?"

"Get up. Let me lay down." Zach yanked Brandon's arm. As he lay on his back and spread his legs, he said, "Cover your dick with this shit and shove it up my ass."

"What?" Brandon gasped.

"Just do it!"

Trying to stop trembling, Brandon did what he was told.

"You sure?"

"Hurry, you idiot!"

Looking quickly back at the door, Brandon pushed into Zach's anus and felt his skin explode with chills.

"Pump! Pump!" Zach urged quietly.

Slightly shocked by the act, he needed the encouragement. Brandon began thrusting his hips into Zach's body. The surge of power from the penetration shook him to the core. When he came he almost passed out. "Ah!"

"Shh!" Zach warned, disconnecting their bodies. Sitting up, gaping at Brandon, Zach gushed, "You believe it? You believe what that felt like?"

"*Holy shit!*" Brandon enunciated slowly.

"You think that's what gay guys do? Huh? Brandy? You think that's how they have sex?"

"*Holy shit…*"

"We need to get decent. I have no doubt Shandy will be looking for us." Zach climbed off the bed, capped the jar of petroleum jelly, and stood still. "Your spunk is running down my leg," he laughed.

Brandon hopped off the bed, standing beside him, waiting. "Yours too. How weird is that?"

"Come on. Let's clean up and get back to the party."

"Oh, Zach…I don't know how you do it, but you are incredible."

As he wiped himself off with some toilet tissue, Zach replied, "I got news for you, Brandy, now that we know how to do it, we'll never want to stop. The only problem is, where are we going to do it again?"

"I don't know, Zach. But, one day, one day when we're grown up and have a job. We can live together and do it every night and day."

Pausing, smiling at him, Zach spit on his palm and held it

out. "Best friends."

Brandon spit on his hand and clasped Zach's. "Bestest friends."

The party had gone completely out of control. Lamps were being knocked over and smashed, beer spilled on sofa cushions and carpets. Zach and Brandon had one look at the chaos and shook their heads sadly.

"Where the heck did you guys disappear to?" Shandy asked, her make-up smeared, slurring her words. "I made out with Truman...ha ha."

"He's welcome to you," Zach sneered.

"Don't go," Shandy whined.

"Ew." Brandon shivered in exaggeration as he stared at her drunken face. "Let's get out of here."

Moving past the crammed bodies in the living room, Zach made it to the front door, grabbing Brandon to come out behind him. A moment after they walked up the street, two patrol cars pulled in front of the house.

Gaping in shock, Zach said, "That was too close for comfort."

"Man, my dad would have killed me." Brandon nudged Zach to keep moving away so they wouldn't be associated with the party.

Once they were a few blocks from the noise, Zach stopped Brandon and smiled at him. "That was the most amazing thing I have ever done."

Sighing adoringly, Brandon replied, "Me, too."

Peeking around the darkness, Zach pulled Brandon to his lips and kissed him passionately. Hearing Brandon moan in pleasure was so satisfying. Parting, looking around again, Zach said, "I can't wait until we have our own place."

"Me neither. Christ, Zach, it can't happen fast enough."

"Three more months and we're in college. It'll happen, Brandy. It'll get here." Zach put his arm around Brandon's waist as they walked back to the well-lit main street.

"Yeah, soon. Very soon." Brandon sighed wistfully.

Feeling the excitement of a life together burning in his chest, Zach inhaled the cooler night air.

Chapter Nine

Brandon descended the stairs with a light, bouncy gait. As he moved through the ground floor of the house, he heard his mother talking on the phone in the kitchen. Walking in, seeing her seated on a chair at the table, Brandon poured himself a glass of orange juice and tuned in to her conversation.

"Okay, Maude…yes. I think it would be great fun. I'll talk to Mel about it. No, he's due some time off. Yes…I don't know. Even if Reece came home for a few weeks, I don't think he'd be interested. He's too old for that kind of thing."

Brandon had no idea what she was planning with Zach's mom. He sat down at the table near her, looking straight at her asking silently for a clue. She met his eye, smiled, but didn't give anything away.

"Great. Yes. No, you go ahead and make the reservations. I don't see any problem. I'll call Mel at work and get back to you. The summers are slow for him anyway, it's the best time for him to take time off. Great. Okay, Maude, let me go and call him. Bye, now." She hung up and gave Brandon a big grin.

"What's going on?"

"How would you like to go to Florida for a couple of weeks?"

"With Zach's family?"

"Yes."

"Cool." Brandon began imagining the possibilities of an empty hotel room.

"Let me call your father to see if he can take the time off."

"When? When are we thinking of going?"

"The last week in July, the first week in August." She dialed the phone.

"Great. I'm headed to Memorial Pool. Okay?"

"No breakfast?" She held up her hand to say into the phone, "Honey, it's me."

Brandon whispered, "I'll catch something there."

"Hold on, Mel, Brandon is talking to me." She cupped the phone. "Take some cash out of my purse. I should have a five in there."

"Thanks, see ya later." Brandon finished his juice, placing his glass in the sink. Before he left he heard his mother say to his father, "It'll be fun. When was the last time we went to Florida?"

Zach slouched in the high metal chair, sunglasses on his nose, a baseball cap on his head, and a whistle around his neck. It was early in the day and only three lifeguards were on duty before the crowds grew thick and the water crowded. Yawning, he stretched his back and noticed Shandy standing below him. "You get in trouble last night?" he asked.

Shandy shrugged. "The cops just made everyone leave."

"I bet Zelene's parents killed her when they got home."

"It wasn't her fault. She didn't bring the booze."

Zach laughed, scanning the water again dutifully.

"Where were you?"

"Huh?" He leaned over to see her again. "Where was I?"

"Yeah. Last night. Alyssa and I looked everywhere for you. Where did you disappear to?"

"Uh, some of the guys had booze in the backyard. So, we stepped out to have a few drinks."

"Really? I didn't know anyone was in the backyard."

He shrugged, waiting for a kid to pop up after diving off a board. Seeing him surface, Zach gazed out at the water again. After a minute he looked down at her. "You're still there?"

"Yeah. Why?"

"I thought you made out with Truman. Why don't you go and hang out with him?"

"I only made out with him because I couldn't find you."

"Oh. Too bad." Zach noticed a bicycle rider coming down the sidewalk from Berdan Avenue and wondered if it was Brandon. Seeing Shandy still lingering, he sighed tiredly. In his head he was praying for her to go away.

"How come you didn't want to make out with me at Zelene's?" She climbed up the side of the chair.

Zach peered down at her and said, "Don't do that. I'll get in trouble."

She hopped back to the sand again. "You hate me, don't you? You hate me and you hated high school."

"I don't hate you, but, yes, I hated high school. I'm ready to begin working on my college degree." He looked over at the cyclist and did recognize Brandon as he locked his bike to the fence.

"Where are you going to college?"

"I don't know yet. Look, can you just go away? I need to work."

"Geez, bite my head off." A minute later she announced, "Oh, look, your boyfriend is here."

Knowing Brandon was most likely on his way over, Zach just sneered at her, "Get lost."

Brandon's lip curled in revulsion when he noticed Shandy

standing next to Zach's chair. Dropping his towel on the sand, kicking off his shoes, he tried to decide if he should wait until she left or approach Zach now.

Before Brandon came to a conclusion, Shandy made her way directly over to him. In a snotty voice, she said, "Your boyfriend is waiting for you."

"Shut up," Brandon replied.

Turning up her nose in defiance, Shandy walked away.

That cold pit came to Brandon's stomach. Pausing so it wouldn't seem as if he was desperate to talk to Zach, Brandon plopped down on his towel to fume.

Zach twisted around in his chair, looking for him.

Seeing him, Brandon gave him a slight wave. Zach acknowledged him with a wave back. Checking the clock on the building behind him, reading it was five minutes to the hour, Brandon hoped Zach would be relieved and come over to him first so he wouldn't be accused of anything. "Oh, fuck this..." he grumbled and stood, walking over to his lover.

"Why the hell did you take so long?" Zach asked.

"Stupid Shandy said something."

"Screw her."

"When is your break?" Brandon asked, shading his eyes as he looked up at him.

"Five minutes."

"Good. You mind if I wait on my towel. I can't stand the thought of Shandy glaring at me."

"Okay." Zach looked back at the first aid hut.

When Brandon turned to where Zach was staring, he found another lifeguard coming his way. "Oh. Here's your guy now."

As the changing of the guard took place, Brandon looked around the area again for any sign of prying eyes.

Zach nodded for Brandon to walk to his towel. They both sat down on it.

"I wanted to tell you that my mom and your mom are planning a trip to Florida for us."

Zach brightened up. "Yeah?"

"Yeah. The last week in July, first week in August."

"You think they'll let us share a hotel room together?"

Imagining the possibility, Brandon asked, "You mean, just me and you?"

Zach shrugged. "Why not? Where else are we gonna stay? With our parents?"

"Zach that would be so fricken awesome. I don't even want to get my hopes up because I'll go nuts if it doesn't happen."

"Let me talk to my mom. Think about it, Brandy. Most likely your parents will want a room to themselves."

"What about Hannah?"

"She can sleep in my parents' room. I'm not sharing a room with her."

"I hope you're right. Can you imagine that? Two weeks? Us alone in a hotel room?" Brandon felt his heart race wildly. "Oh, this is too cool!"

"Fingers crossed, Brandy, fingers crossed. Let me take a piss. I have to get back on duty in a few minutes."

"Okay." Brandon thought about the potential of being alone in a bedroom with Zach. It was too good to be true.

After taking a dip, waiting for Zach to be finished with his shift so they could go home together, Brandon sat impatiently on his towel drying off before he stepped into his shorts again. Patches of thick clouds obscured the hot sun, threatening a quick thundershower where they lingered. The head lifeguard seemed to be assessing the situation and at the first sound of a rumble, he instructed the guards to clear the pool. Standing to watch, Brandon waited as Zach stood in his chair and blew the whistle in blasts, waving the bathers out of the water.

Brandon put on his t-shirt just as a few raindrops pelted his back. Most of the crowd began packing up, racing for their cars or the shelter of the overhanging buildings before the teaming rain started. As Brandon rolled up his towel, Zach raced over to him, his head down to avoid the large spattering drops.

"This way!" Zach waved.

Brandon raced behind him to the first aid hut. Huddled with a small group of people, looking out at the large lake with its dark, ominous storm cloud, Brandon whispered, "You almost done?"

"Yeah. Let me give them their whistle. I think they'll probably close the pool for a few hours until this passes."

Brandon watched as he disappeared into a room emerging a moment later wearing his shorts and shirt. "We should wait until it lets up a little. We'll get soaked riding home in this."

Brandon nodded, standing shoulder to shoulder with him as everyone seemed to be deciding what to do for the best in the deluge.

As the time ticked by and no change appeared in the weather, Brandon grew antsy. "Let's just go for it."

"You sure?" Zach asked.

"Yeah. What's the difference if you're wet from swimming or wet from the rain?"

"I just don't want to get zapped!" Zach laughed, ducking in reflex when another crack of thunder rumbled in the angry sky.

"The tires are rubber. We're grounded." Brandon waved excitedly. "Come on!"

Laughing wildly as they raced to their bicycles, they unlocked them, and by the time they were mounted and moving, they were already drenched. Brandon could hear Zach's mixture of cursing and chuckling as he fought to see in the teaming sheet of water.

Standing on his pedals, Brandon pumped his legs as hard as he could up the incline towards home.

By the time the arrived at their houses, they were completely saturated. Brandon jumped off his bike and carried it up to his porch as Zach did the same next door. Through the rain Brandon yelled, "Shower and meet here or there?"

"Here!"

Waving, Brandon stepped into his living room and tried to use his soaked towel to dab off the dripping water from his face and hair.

"What on earth?" Lois stood in front of him, shaking her head. "Why didn't you wait for it to let up?"

"We tried. It was taking too long."

"Let me get you a dry towel." She took the wet one and gingerly carried it to the laundry, returning with a fresh one.

Brandon rubbed it over his head and down his arms. "I'm just going to shower quickly and then go to Zach's."

"Oh? Is he done working for the day?"

"Yes." He handed her back the towel and dashed up to the second floor.

"We're having his parents over for dinner tonight," she yelled up the stairs after him, "to discuss the travel plans!"

"Okay!" he shouted back, grinning, stripping for a hot shower.

Dressed in clean, dry clothing, Zach found his mother reading in the den. "Mom?"

She raised her head and smiled at him.

He sat down near her, on the arm of the sofa, and looked down at the romance novel on her lap first before he asked, "Can I talk to you for a sec?"

"Sure, Zachary. What's on your mind? Work okay?"

"Yeah, it's easy money. I enjoy it."

"Good." She placed a bookmark on her page and closed the paperback.

"Uh...Brandon mentioned we're all going to Florida together."

"Yes. Will you be able to take time off?"

"Oh, don't worry about it. But I...I wanted to ask you about the room set up." He bit his lip and tried his best to make it sound innocent.

"Room set up?"

"You know, at the hotel and stuff."

"Oh? What about it?"

Zach looked at the front cover of her book. It was a picture of a man and woman, and the low-cut Victorian gown on the woman showed off cleavage. Zach cleared his throat and hoped the images of sex in the novel she was just reading wouldn't taint her opinion. "Well, I was thinking you and Dad would obviously share a room..."

"I get it."

He paused and asked, "You do?"

"You don't want to be with Hannah."

"No, I don't. I'll be turning eighteen soon, and she's a pest. I was thinking...maybe...me and Brandon could share a room, if it's not too expensive. And maybe, Hannah could stay with you and Dad? Please, Mom?"

A wry smile came to her face, and Zach tried not to read anything into it. If Hannah had opened her mouth about what she had seen he and Brandon doing that day, now was the moment he would find out.

"How does Brandon feel about it? Did you ask him if he minded sharing a room with you?"

"I did. He doesn't. He said he thought it would be better that way. You know. We would most likely hang out together and go off on our own a little, and we wouldn't bother you if we came and went a lot. Does that make sense?"

"Go off on your own? In Florida?"

Zach cursed himself for overstepping slightly. "I don't mean like all night. I assumed you meant for us to go to Disney World or SeaWorld or something together, so we'll all be a group then. I just meant once we were back at the hotel, like if we wanted to swim or something…" He felt sweat break out on his forehead. Was he babbling too much?

"I don't want you boys going off on your own." A stern expression appeared on her face.

"All right. We won't, but I still would appreciate the privacy of us having our own space."

A strange light came to her eyes. Zach died inside. He cursed the stupid romance novels for giving her the wrong impression, or the right one. "Why are you looking at me like that?"

"Why do you and Brandon need the privacy of your own space?"

"Mom," he groaned, "We're guys. We don't want our parents or my kid sister hanging around."

The look of suspicion didn't change. Zach suddenly wondered if he hadn't said a word, if the division of rooms would have fallen to what they desired naturally and he was screwing it all up by using the wrong verbiage to get what he desperately needed.

Then, to his absolute horror, she asked in a very quiet voice, "Is there something you need to tell me?"

Instantly, he felt ill. Standing up, knowing anything he said from that point on wouldn't be interpreted well, Zach replied, "Never mind. You guys will do what you want anyway."

"Zachary," she called after him.

Waving goodbye to her, he left the house and felt like vomiting he was so sick about it.

The Boy Next Door

Brandon was just about to jog next door when he found Zach on his porch. He opened the screen door and said, "Oh. Wasn't I supposed to come to your place?"

Zach nudged him inside, looking around first before he headed up the stairs to Brandon's bedroom.

His smile falling at Zach's expression, Brandon followed him up and closed the door. When they were both standing near Brandon's bed, Brandon asked, "What's wrong?"

"I think I fucked up." Zach dropped down on the mattress and hung his head.

"How?" Brandon sat next to him.

"I was just trying to get Mom to let us share a room together. I don't know how it came out, but she started getting all weird on me."

"Weird how?" Brandon felt that icy chill again.

"Like asking me why we needed to be alone and shit. I told her it was because in case we went off on our own, and that backfired. Then I said we wanted privacy, and she got all suspicious on me. I swear, Brandy, no matter what I said she had this look on her face that was really fricken scary."

"You don't think…" Brandon shook his head in denial.

"I don't know what to think. She actually asked me if I had something to tell her. I shit a brick, Brandy."

Brandon sat still, mulling it over. "Hannah must have told her."

"You think? I figured if she did, then Mom would have just said so. You know, accused me."

"Why would she just come to the conclusion we were? No way, Zach. You must have read her wrong. She most likely just thinks we'll get up to something, like drinking, or sneaking out."

"You know the stupid part?" Zach turned to face him. "I

think if I didn't say anything, they most likely would have just stuck us together anyway. I mean, where would we sleep? With our parents?"

"I wish we were older, and we didn't have to play by anyone's rules but our own." Brandon snuck a touch of Zach's thigh.

Boldly, Zach clasped his hand over it. "I know. I just feel sick that she might think we're gay, Brandy. I'm so pissed at myself."

"You know your parents are coming here for dinner tonight to talk about the plans."

"No. Are they?"

"Yes. So, we can hang around and see what exactly they intend on doing. I'm sure if we stick to our guns, they'll let us share a room together. Believe me, your mom can't think that of us. No way."

"Yes, way! I'm almost eighteen and I've only brought one ugly girl home once to go to the senior prom. Duh!"

"Stop it. Cut it out, Zach." Brandon felt queasy.

Another loud thunderclap rumbled outside, a flash of lightning followed. Brandon stood up and peered out at the gray day. It was raining so hard the streets were flooded and water was flowing down the sewers in waves. Feeling warmth next to him, Brandon looked over at Zach who was staring out at the torrent.

"I want to be in a room with you, Brandy. So bad I ache."

"Me too. Don't worry. Even if they try to separate us, we'll sneak off. They can't stop us."

A smile finally edged out the sadness in Zach's face. "Right. We'll manage."

"Yup."

Another lightning bolt cut through the black sky. Together they counted, "One-one-thousand-two-two-thousand..." and the thunder shook the house.

A group of seven sat around the large oblong dining room table in Brandon's house. His mother carried loaded dishes of food with serving spoons poking out of them, placing them in the center so everyone could help themselves. It was like Thanksgiving had shown up in June. The storm still crackled outdoors and the air conditioning felt slightly chilly as it blew overhead. Zach licked his lips at the savory selections and piled his plate high when the platters came his way. Low chatter from small conversations rattled around the table until everyone was stuffing their faces and sipping the wine or soda pop.

After a few moments to enjoy the good food, Mel began the conversation they had all gathered to discuss. "Non-stop flights from Newark to Orlando."

"Check," Sly replied, nodding.

"And the hotel? Is it near Disney World?"

Sly finished chewing his food and replied, "It's in Kissimmee. Very close to both Disney World and SeaWorld. I've reserved a minivan with eight seats."

"Great!" Lois nodded.

Brandon and Zach exchanged glances. Then Brandon asked boldly, "Er, how many rooms?"

Sly responded casually, "Three. Hannah will stay with us."

"Goody!" she giggled.

Zach and Brandon looked at each other again. Finally, Zach got up the courage to glance at his mother. She had been staring at him during the conversation. Before Zach asked her, Maude answered "You and Brandon will share a room."

Zach felt his cheeks go crimson. It was as if she was privy to his private thoughts. Did she know? Did she suspect? *Oh, God help me.*

Brandon sipped his cola and said, "Cool."

"How are we driving to the airport?" Lois asked.

Sly replied, "I've gotten us a lift with Airport Express. It was much cheaper than the airport parking lot."

"This is so rad!" Hannah chirped happily. "I've always wanted to go to Disney World."

Zach felt Brandon kick his shoe. Looking up sheepishly, he caught Brandon's glistening eyes. Quickly, Zach peeked at his mother to see if she caught the exchange. She was busy eating again, nodding, smiling, and answering questions. Zach shook his head at Brandon in admonishment, trying to convey to him to keep silent about it. Brandon's glee faded.

When the dinner plates were removed and an apple pie and chocolates were set out with a pot of coffee, Zach met Brandon by the front living room window as they checked to see if the rain had finally stopped. Before he said anything, Zach glanced over his shoulder, whispering into Brandon's ear, "We did it."

"I can't believe we have two weeks in a hotel room, alone."

"I could spurt thinking about it."

"Boys," Lois asked, "would you like some dessert?"

Exchanging wicked grins, Zach and Brandon nodded to her enthusiastically.

As the evening wound down and it became late, and the conversations mixed with yawns, Zach said goodnight to Brandon, exchanging a secret wink. The Shermans waved to the Townsend clan and walked next door.

Zach felt his mother's arm come to rest around his shoulders. He looked over at her and caught her knowing smile. "What?"

"I just want you both to behave yourselves."

"Come on, Ma. What could we do that we don't do here? We're not juvenile delinquents."

"No. You're not. You're both very good boys."

The Boy Next Door

Sly opened the front door for them. Hannah ran in first with Maude and Zach behind her, Sly last, closing the door again.

"You mind staying in a room with Brandon, Zach?" Sly asked.

"Mind? No. Why would I? He's my best friend."

"Good. I just didn't know how you felt about it." Zach looked at his mother in confusion. It dawned on him the suspicions she had she was keeping close to her chest. "It's fine, Dad."

Sly paused before he left the room, saying, "This is probably the last summer vacation you'll have with the family. I know when I turned eighteen I wasn't interested in it anymore. I suspect neither will you."

"Don't say that, Sly," Maude admonished. "He's still my little boy." She hugged Zach.

Zach smiled and hugged her back. "Thanks, Mom. I'll be going to bed now. I have an early shift at the pool in the morning."

"Goodnight, Zach," she whispered, kissing his cheek.

He kissed her back and waved to his dad, then climbed the stairs tiredly. Could he tell her? Or would that be asking for trouble?

Chapter Ten

The flight was long, annoying, and the plane felt like a can of sardines. The ride from the airport in Orlando to Kissimmee seemed to take forever with everyone shouting directions and opinions, all the while Hannah was whining she had to pee. The check-in at the hotel was enough to bring one to tears the line was so long. It seemed everyone in America thought Florida in July was a good idea.

"And we thought New Jersey was hot!" Brandon blew out a gust of wind in frustration as sweat dripped down his nose. He was trying to feel cool in the air conditioned lobby.

"Almost there," Zach mumbled under his breath as they closed in on the check-in counter at the lush hotel.

Brandon watched both sets of parents leaning over towards the staff, credit cards in their hands. A mountain of luggage was being loaded on a wheelie cart. Two bellboys led the way onto an elevator, and suddenly, Brandon and Zachary were being shown to their private room. Two bags were left inside with them and silence followed the clamor of voices as the rest of the family was shown down the hall to their prospective rooms.

Brandon held his breath. Zach stared at him with wide eyes. As the noise of the crowd petered out, Zach whispered, "Did we do it?"

Brandon burst out laughing. Nodding his head, he gasped, "We did it!"

The Boy Next Door

They raced towards each other and embraced, taking turns lifting each other off their feet. Brandon laughed so hard he was in tears. Zach was in the same state. Then a knock was heard on their door.

Separating, wiping their eyes and making sure they looked serious, Zach opened the door. His mother stood there.

"We'll meet for dinner in about an hour. Everyone wants to just rest for a little while after all the traveling."

Zach nodded, responding flatly, "Okay."

"So, about five? Come to our room?"

"Okay."

She looked over her son's shoulder to Brandon. He tried to give her a polite nod and smile. In a stern voice she warned, "Behave yourselves."

"We will, Mom." Zach looked directly into her face, as if making his point.

Without another word she left. Zach closed the door and turned around slowly. "She fucking knows."

"You don't know that." Brandon sat on one of the single beds.

"I can tell. I feel really weird about it."

"Oh?" Brandon felt slightly let down. "So, now you don't want to share a room?"

"No! Don't be stupid."

"I'm taking a shower. I'm a sweaty mess." Brandon scuffed his feet to the bathroom and scoped out the facilities. Staring at the little soaps, tiny bottles of shampoo and lotion, he unbuttoned his shirt, dropping it to the floor. In the mirror he could see Zach coming in.

Stepping back as Zach used the toilet, Brandon finished undressing and started the shower holding his hand out to test to the temperature. When Zach was through urinating, he stripped as well. Brandon stood under the cool spray and grinned wickedly when Zach joined him. They closed the glass sliding door and took turns wetting down under the refreshing water. Brandon unwrapped one of the little bars of soap and began lathering his chest. Zach's eyes were connected to his hands. Brandon moved the soap lower, washing his genitals. Zach's eyes followed his every move.

"Oh, this is really too good to be true," Brandon laughed, his voice echoing off the wet tiles.

"Give me that."

Brandon handed Zach the bar of soap. Moving closer, Zach began washing Brandon's cock for him, lathering it up and making it slippery in his palms. Brandon groaned in pleasure, bracing himself with a hand on the wall and a hand on the door, spreading his legs wide. Covered in soap, Zach moved his right hand up and down Brandon's cock, and with his left he massaged his balls, pushing his index finger up Brandon's ass. Brandon shivered and arched his back, thrusting his hips forward, begging for more. A feeling as strong as a convulsion rocked Brandon it was so intense. Letting out a sound in ecstasy, Brandon clenched his jaw and closed his eyes as come shot out of his body with an orgasm so strong he thought he may pass out. With Zach continuing to massage him inside and out, the sensation Brandon experienced was slow to subside. Moving his cock in and out of Zach's palm, like a slow motion pole-dancer, Brandon finally opened his eyes as if waking from a deep sleep.

Zach was smiling demonically at him. "Oh, man, I can tell that was a good one."

"Jesus, Zach…it feels better up my ass with the soap. It definitely needs something slippery in there. Like it did with the stuff we used at the party."

"I know." Zach continued to toy with Brandon gently.

"We need baby oil, petroleum jelly, or something."

"We'll get some. My turn?"

"Yeah." Brandon moved so Zach could lean against the back wall and hold onto the door as he had done. Soaping up to a frothing lather, Brandon gave Zach exactly what he had received; one hand jerking his cock, the other between his legs, probing. Instantly, Zach's mouth opened to his intake of sharp, deep breaths. "Oh, Brandy, Brandy..."

"Is it good?" Brandon whispered, the words echoing off the walls. Licking his lips, loving the expression on Zach's face, Brandon pushed in deeper, feeling the back of Zach's scrotum and massaging it, knowing what that felt like. Zach's body tensed and his hips thrust forward in reflex. When the come shot out of him, it hit Brandon in the stomach so hard it was like a pellet gun. "Wow."

Zach struggled to open his eyes, his knees giving out under him. "Holy mother fucking shit..."

"I'm telling ya—baby oil." Brandon rinsed off his genitals under the spray. When he attempted to turn around to face Zach, Zach grabbed him from behind and jammed his hips against Brandon's bottom playfully.

"When I get oil on my dick, I'm going to stick it in you so hard..." Zach sucked in a deep inhale of air.

"Oh yes!" Brandon laughed. "I can't believe we have two weeks of this!"

"It's a dream, Brandy. A fucking dream."

"I just hope it never ends. When we get to college and share a room, it'll be great." Brandon tried to locate Zach's mouth, leaning back for it.

Zach stretched over Brandon's shoulder and found it. Once they connected tongues, Brandon twisted to face Zach. Wrapped tightly around each other, their lips glued together, Brandon was in heaven. Absolute heaven.

Sitting in the hotel's fine restaurant, dressed in their good clothing, Brandon and Zach tried their best not to gulp their food in order to end the night and get into bed together. Zach had already investigated the gift shop and spotted baby oil on the shelf. They just needed a minute alone to buy it.

When Lois suggested a nice long stroll to walk off their dinner, the boys had to reluctantly agree or risk too many questions. Zach kept getting unnerving glances from his mother and he didn't want to cause her to suspect them anymore than she already did.

By nine o'clock Hannah was yawning and rubbing her eyes and everyone seemed to be running out of steam. Strolling leisurely back to the hotel, Zach cursed under his breath to find the shop had closed. On the door was a sign with their opening hours. He had to wait until eight in the morning for his baby oil.

Kissing his mother goodnight, enduring her long look, Zach waved, trying not to smile too brightly as he and Brandon once again were left alone in their private room. Zach made sure the extra lock was secure on the door and the curtain was drawn over the window. He found Brandon taking off his good shirt and slacks after turning on the television with a remote control.

"I am so tired." Brandon yawned.

"Me, too. That stupid shop is closed."

"Hmm?" Brandon peeled back the bedspread of one of the twin beds.

"Baby oil. I have to get it tomorrow."

"Oh."

"You want to push the beds together?"

"Sure. We just have to remember to push them apart again in the morning."

"We will." Zach stood on the outside of the single bed and nudged it until it attached to Brandon's.

Brandon had stripped down to his briefs and then collapsed on the bed, his eyes drooping.

The Boy Next Door

Taking off all his clothing, Zach crawled over the bed to cuddle with Brandon. Stuffing his hand down the front of Brandon's briefs, Zach snuggled against Brandon's back and looked at the television from over his shoulder. Within a few minutes he could hear Brandon's deep breathing. Smiling to himself, he whispered, "Goodnight, Brandy." He shut off the light and television, returning to his spot, spooning Brandon from behind, his hand inside Brandon's underwear, cupping his genitals.

Chapter Eleven

The sound of someone knocking at their door startled them. Zach sat up as if he had a spring on his bed. "Shit! Brandy!"

Stirring, Brandon woke, heard the knocking, then Maude's voice on the other end calling, "Wake up, boys!"

Jumping off the beds, separating them, they both slipped into their shorts and tried to tame their wild bed-hair before opening the door. Zach checked with Brandon. Brandon nodded in readiness waiting for Zach to answer that door. Clearing his throat, Zach opened it and casually said, "Oh, hi, Mom."

Peering into the room, Maude seemed desperate to get inside, but Zach stood in her way. "We were going to go to the pancake house for breakfast and then head to Disney World."

"Okay." Zach ran his hand through his hair and nodded, keeping calm. "Give us an hour. We just woke up."

"An hour?"

Zach felt her pushing the door back against his side. Reluctantly, he allowed her to enter the room. Like a police inspector, she investigated every aspect of the furnishings and bed linens. Zach knew it was unnerving Brandon and hoped his lover was doing nothing to give away their nighttime activities behind his back.

"How about a half hour?" she asked. "Good morning,

Brandon. Did you sleep well?"

"Yes, Mrs. Sherman."

Zach looked over his shoulder at Brandon. He seemed calm. Standing still. His arms at his sides. Nothing to be suspicious about.

"Half hour?" Maude asked her son again.

"Okay." Zach nodded.

She took one last look at the unmade beds, then left. Zach closed the door, exhaling a deep breath.

"Geez, Zach," Brandon whispered, "I swear she suspects something."

"I know." Zach headed to the bathroom to wash up.

"What the hell are we going to do?" Brandon followed him.

"Nothing. Brandon, we can't do anything." Zach urinated in the toilet, then washed his hands and face, brushing his teeth over the sink.

"Shit. I hope she doesn't discuss it with my mom." Brandon copied Zach's lead in the cleaning up ritual.

"Look, let's not worry about it. I think if my mom really thought something was going on, she'd confront me. She's like that. She wouldn't just think it, she'd say it." Zach left the room to put on fresh clothing.

"Man, do you really think they would hate us if they found out?"

After zipping his shorts, Zach bit his lip as he stared at Brandon's worried expression. "I don't know, Brandy. But, my dad has made some nasty comments in the past about gay guys. I don't think he's too keen on them."

Pausing to think about it, Brandon replied, "I've never heard my dad discuss gay guys. I have no idea what he thinks."

"Believe me. He'll hate you if you tell him." Zach finished dressing then ran his brush through his hair.

After he had tucked in his shirt, Brandon reached for Zach's hairbrush to tame his long, wavy hair. "I wish we didn't have to hide."

As they stood side by side in front of the mirror on the dresser, Zach admired them both in the reflection. "Once we're in college, there's nothing they can do."

"So, we're both going to NYU, right?"

Shrugging, Zach responded, "I suppose."

Brandon tossed the brush down on the dresser, heading to the door.

Zach looked around the room, making sure nothing appeared unusual. He stuffed his wallet and the room key into the pocket of his shorts and closed the door behind them.

Eight hours later, having their fill of rides, greasy food, long lines, boiling temperatures, and high humidity, the weary group made their way back to the hotel.

Zach purposely lagged behind while his and Brandon's family walked past the shop toward their rooms. Hannah was moaning about a stomachache and sunburn as she dragged her feet alongside their parents.

Seeing his opportunity, Zach hit Brandon on the arm, getting his attention. Wearily, Brandon looked back. Zach tilted his head to the shop. It seemed at first that Brandon didn't get it, then he acknowledged Zach.

Right before he opened the shop door, Zach heard his mother ask, "Where are you going?"

Zach cursed under his breath. "Just getting something. Don't worry about it."

Brandon seemed to freeze where he stood.

Maude backtracked until she stood next to him. "Zach, I have everything you could possibly need. At least tell me what it is you're buying. Do you have an upset stomach like

Hannah?"

"No. I'm just getting a magazine. Okay?"

"What kind of magazine?"

That enraged him. Suddenly feeling as though she were treating him like a toddler instead of an eighteen year old, Zach snarled, "A fucking *Playboy*, okay?"

Brandon gasped audibly behind them.

Maude glared at her son, then in a measured voice, she whispered, "You better watch your mouth, Zachary. You're not on your own yet."

"No, but I will be by September. And you know what, Ma? I can't wait."

Behind Maude's back, Brandon was waving his arms furiously. The rest of the group had stopped their progress to their rooms, but were too far away to hear.

Maude narrowed her eyes at Zach. "You think we can't pull the plug, Zachary? Who do you think is paying for your education? You?"

Zach hated her at that moment. Hated being dependent. Yes, he had worked every summer since he was fifteen, but he still only had around four thousand dollars in his savings account. "Pull the plug? Just because I want to buy a magazine?"

"No, because of your attitude. You think I'm stupid, Zachary, but you're very wrong. I know exactly what's going on, and if your father knew, you'd be in very big trouble."

Zach felt his skin crawl. Peeking quickly at Brandon, he could see Brandon's Adam's apple move in his gulp of nervous fear.

Shifting aside when someone tried to get out of the shop, Zach assessed the immediate area and tried to see who could hear the conversation. Only Brandon could at the moment, but he knew his father's curiosity was becoming piqued, and it would take one more minute of debating for him to come over and ask what was going on.

"All right, Mom. You think you know what's going on. Then why not just tell me? What's with all the secrecy?"

"Secrecy?" she laughed sadly. "Oh, Zachary, you're not one to talk of secrecy."

At that moment, Zachary knew she knew. His cocky boldness fell from him like an avalanche. "We can't help it."

"I'm not so sure of that. I think you two *can* help it."

"Mom." Zach realized this argument had indeed taken too long. Sly was now strutting his way over.

"What's going on?" Sly asked.

Zach bit his lip, staring at his mother.

"Nothing," she sighed tiredly. "He just wants to buy a magazine."

"So?" Sly shrugged as if the conversation bordered on absurdity. "Does he need money? You need money, Zachary?" Sly took out his wallet.

"No, Dad. I got it." Zach gave his mother a long agonizing look, then twisted away and entered the shop.

As he did, Zach heard his father ask, "What the hell's the big deal, Maude? So what if the kid wants a magazine?"

Unable to hear his mother's response as they walked away from the storefront, Zach closed his eyes and tried to calm down his jumping insides. He was sick about it.

Brandon touched his arm, whispering quietly, "Zach?"

"She knows."

"I know. What's she going to do about it?"

"I don't know." Zach walked to the front window of the shop to peer out. The group was gone. He picked out a small bottle of baby oil, then a car magazine, and brought them to the counter. He knew Brandon was freaking out, but ignored it for now. Thanking the clerk, taking the plastic bag and the receipt, Zach left the shop with Brandon following behind him. Not a word was spoken until they were inside their room. Once Zach locked the door and tossed the bag on his twin bed, he covered his face and struggled not to become emotional.

Brandon didn't know what to do. Gently, he led Zach to sit down. "Can we talk to her?"

Zach shook his head, wiping at his wet eyes.

"What did she say exactly, Zach? Was she upset? Is she going to tell my parents?"

"She was upset, yes. She didn't make any comment either way on telling anyone, except my dad. But she did say she could pull the plug on my college education."

Scoffing under his breath, Brandon answered, "No way, Zach. She would never do that. She wants you to go to college, so that's an empty threat."

"Brandy, if my dad knew we were screwing each other, he'd disown me."

Brandon felt instantly pale. "No. Zach, no way. Your dad is crazy about you."

"He hates gays, Brandy. I remember some guy on the television who was kind of campy, you know the type. A little feminine?" He bent his wrist in an obvious gesture. "Well, you should have heard my dad. He made it sound as if he wanted to kill the guy."

Brandon was shocked. He knew Sly since he was born. Never in all that time had he ever seen a side to that big man that would indicate that kind of intolerance for anyone. "Maybe he was just joking?"

When Zach tilted his way, Brandon could see the look of seriousness in Zach's eyes. "Okay. Where does that leave us, Zach?"

Leaning over his lap, rubbing his face, Zach moaned, "I don't know."

A wash of loneliness cascaded over Brandon's length. He didn't know? Was there any doubt that they would be together? Forever?

It was too much for Brandon to bear. He stood and took the room key, leaving Zach to his sulking. It was nearing seven and the hotel was busy with patrons, swimming, eating in the fine restaurant, playing tennis, shuffleboard, and ping-pong. Children were screaming, running around wildly. In all the noise, Brandon heard nothing. On the periphery of the crowd he felt alone. As he scuffed his heels, he found a secluded spot beyond the two pools. There was a grassy patch with a white iron bench and a palm tree swaying hypnotically, all on its own. Seated on the hot metal, Brandon crouched over his knees and leaned his chin in his palm. A life without Zachary wasn't possible. No. They had a scheme. They would go to the same college, stay in the same dorm room. After they graduated they would get an apartment together. That was the plan. If that plan fell apart, there was no other.

A volcano of emotion was just under the surface. Battling with it to keep it capped, not explode into wailing sobs, Brandon bit his lip. He was already overwhelmed with the idea of college, finding a career he could tolerate, leaving home, being independent... It was already too much. No. He needed Zach to be by his side. Together they could deal with everything. But not alone. No. That wasn't the plan.

As the sky grew tinged with dusk and the mosquitoes became hungry, Brandon motivated himself to go back to the room. Shuffling his exhausted legs towards their private domain, he thought only of a cool shower and sleep. Using his key in the door, he cracked it open, found it dim inside, and entered. Zach was under a light sheet, seemingly asleep. Closing the door quietly, Brandon headed to the bathroom and stripped for a shower. The entire time he was washing up, he kept waiting for Zach to come in, climb behind him in the refreshing water and for them to make love. It never happened.

The Boy Next Door

Coming out of the steam-filled bathroom, a towel around his hips, Brandon hovered over the bed Zach slept on. The two twin mattresses weren't pushed together. There was a gaping space between them. A canyon. A crevasse.

Should he crawl onto the twin behind Zach? Would he suddenly be rejected? Shoved out? Topple to the floor?

He wanted Zach. Needed him.

Walking to the door quietly, Brandon made certain the bolt was secure on it, so no one could enter without them allowing it. Next he moved to the window to adjust the thick curtain, creating a private unit. Determined not to ever give up on their relationship, Brandon dropped his towel on the floor, then pushed his twin bed to meet the other. The room was dim, some noise from a television set could be heard through the wall from the room next door, but other than that, there was nothing to disturb the peace inside their cozy castle. Creeping so he was resting behind Zach on the bed, he slowly embraced him bringing his hips to meet Zach's bottom, his arms to wrap around Zach's waist, pushing his face into Zach's long, dark hair. Brandon yearned for that comfort desperately. Just as he closed his eyes to finally give in to a much needed night's sleep, he felt Zachary stir.

Wondering if the push off, the shove of rejection was inevitable, Brandon held his breath.

As if he, too, was in dire need of reassurance, Zach spun around to face Brandon on the bed. Gripping him, holding him so tightly Brandon could barely breathe or move, Zach hugged him, wrapping his arms and legs around Brandon's body. Then, to Brandon's anguish, he heard Zachary sob. Soon after the muffled sound of his cries, Zach's body began to shake with his wailing. Brandon's heart broke. Moving the sheets so that they had nothing but skin-to-skin contact, Brandon kissed Zach's face, his neck, his jaw, digging his hands through Zachary's thick hair. "They won't tear us apart. Never."

As if hearing what he needed to hear, Zach finally met

Brandon's eyes. Brandon died at the pain he found in them. When Zach's mouth connected to his, Brandon kissed him with as much love and devotion as he could show in that simple act, which in realty, wasn't simple at all. Rocking him side to side on the tiny twin mattress, Brandon wiped Zach's tears away from his cheeks, sucking on his mouth and tongue as if nothing else mattered. And in Brandon's mind, nothing else did.

Chapter Twelve

The last day of their two weeks in Florida had arrived. Packing their things into their suitcases, making sure they had everything they came with, Zach opened and closed drawers and closets mechanically, even though he had done it already. Behind him Brandon was sitting on his suitcase trying to get it zipped.

Finally convinced they had left nothing behind, Zach stared at Brandon as he tried to seal his overstuffed case. "Well, back to reality."

"I know. I got used to sleeping in the same bed as you." Brandon struggled with the zipper, shouting in exasperation, "Can you help me or what?"

Zach hurried over and squashed down the bulging sides of the soft case. "Why did you buy so much?"

"I didn't. Just an extra t-shirt or two. Nothing too big."

"Christ, Brandy!" Zach began moving the strained zipper closer to the end.

Once they had accomplished the task, Zach sat back on his heels and blew out a breath as Brandon rested on the closed luggage. Zach stood and looked out of the window of the room to see if anyone was waiting for them yet.

Brandon joined him, standing next to him, reaching to hold his hand. "Back to sneaking."

"Back to sneaking." Zach's eyes softly focused on the view of one of the pools down below their floor.

Brandon tugged at his arm. Zach turned to see his gentle smile. Feeling affectionate towards him, Zach pecked his cheek quickly. When he gazed back out of the window, he found his father standing in front of it. The look on his face was homicidal.

Zach died.

Brandon choked, "Oh shit."

Instantly, pounding rattled their door and the roar of Sly's deep powerful voice, "Open this door now!"

Zach had lost feeling in his body. He couldn't move.

Brandon whimpered, "What should I do?"

Louder banging ensued.

"Zach?" Brandon cried in panic.

Moving like a zombie, Zach took one step at a time to that door and the fury behind it. Trying to be brave, he opened it.

The smack came so quickly neither boy was prepared.

Tripping back from its power, feeling the burning sting on his face, Zach reached behind him to stop falling as the front door slammed and a mad bull confronted him. Before the next punch came, Sly snarled, "Get out!" to Brandon.

At first Brandon hesitated like he needed to stand between Zach's maniac of a father and Zach.

But Zach knew Brandon would have no chance against his dad. A man so big and powerful he could crush a beer can flat with one swipe. Brandon had waited too long. Sly made a move to throw him out. After one look back at Zach, Brandon left. Zach watched him running past the window.

Alone, Zach waited for the inevitable.

Sly approached him menacingly, face to face in height, but certainly not in girth. Through clenched teeth, he growled, "Tell me I didn't see what I just saw."

The Boy Next Door

Zach knew anything he uttered would not be heard or understood. So he kept silent, but never moved his bold stare from his father's steel blue eyes.

As his volume increased, Sly continued, "*Tell me I didn't see what I just saw*! Tell me I was mistaken! Tell me my son isn't a fucking faggot!"

Zach shivered, but didn't say a word. His father grabbed his throat and Zach was almost lifted off the floor.

"How could you do this to me?" Sly roared, "How could you and Brandon do this behind my back? Behind everyone's back! What the hell are you?"

Zach struggled to swallow with those fingers digging into his trachea. He never raised his arms to defend himself. He knew damn well it would be useless. And besides, his father was dying for an excuse to throttle him. If he so much as flinched, he would be thrown across the room.

A flash passed the window. Next Zach heard his mother's voice. "Sly. Sly, put him down."

As the sound of that calm voice finally reached him, Sly released Zach's throat. Zach rubbed his neck, trying to stop the pain.

"He's a queer, Maude! He's fucking Brandon!"

"I know."

When she said those two words, Sly turned his attention to her like she was the new target.

Outside the window, Brandon and his parents were heading their way, Hannah being instructed to wait outside, which she ignored.

The moment Brandon's parents showed their faces in that room, Sly pointed at them rudely. "Your faggot son corrupted my Zachary!"

Mel pointed back at him in an identical gesture. "Don't you dare accuse my son of anything!"

Turning to face Zach, then to glare at Brandon, Sly screamed, "What the hell were you two doing together in this room all week?"

It was so loud, Zach felt like covering his ears. He was shutting down. He couldn't answer, couldn't look anyone in the eye, and certainly couldn't think.

Before Sly connected another slap to Zachary's cheek, three adults stood in the way. Maude begged her husband to calm down, while Lois comforted Zachary.

Brandon stood alone, wiping his tears as Hannah shouted suddenly, "I saw Zachary put his hand down Brandon's pants!"

The look on Sly's face was so volatile, the room went cold as ice. Sly lunged for Zachary with both fists as three people tried to hold him back. "I'll kill you! You did this perversion in front of your little sister? I'll kill you!"

Lois gripped Zach's numb arm and shoved him outside the room. "Go! Get lost! Let us calm him down."

Zach felt the pushing but comprehended nothing. Brandon touched his shoulder. When he did, Sly went ballistic, foaming at the mouth, screaming so all of the hotel could hear, "Don't you ever touch my son again! You disgusting faggot! Get the hell away from my son!"

Zachary shifted his legs, walking, but didn't feel them move.

Once the boys were gone and Hannah was shooed away, Lois gripped Sly by the shoulders and made him look into her eyes. "Sly! Sly, get a hold of yourself!"

As if it took a supreme effort, Sly met her eyes.

"You listen to me, Sly. We've all been friends for a very long time. You know the boys are close, so that's no surprise."

Sly went to speak in his defense, but Lois stopped him. "Maude and I suspected something, but we kept it to ourselves." Lois gave Mel a quick glance, knowing she had kept it from him as well, then continued, "But, we know this is a phase the boys are going through. Think about it, Sly. They are very comfortable together. It's not scary to be together. But in no way has this decided their sexuality as adults. So stop reacting like an animal and see this for what it is. An adolescent phase."

Sly seemed to take a breath.

In shock, Mel asked his wife, "Lois, what do you mean you and Maude suspected the boys? Why didn't you say anything?"

"Because..." Lois threw up her hands as if it were obvious. "Mel, think about it. You know your reaction would be close to Sly's. You both would think that just because they may have touched each other that they are now branded homosexuals. Nonsense! They're young. They have experimented. That's all there is to it."

"That's the biggest load of crap I have ever heard," Sly snapped. "I never experimented with another boy. You're deluded!"

"Sly, calm down," Maude insisted. "Getting violent and beating Zachary won't do any good."

"They are to be separated from now on, do you hear me? Zachary is going off to Boston to college. That's it!" Sly waved his hands. "No more contact between the two of them! And you three better cooperate or I'll send Zachary to boot camp, you got that?"

Lois exchanged sad looks with her husband.

"Come on, we've got a plane to catch, Sly." Maude tapped her husband's arm. "But, I'm warning you, Sly. Leave the boy alone. You've done enough damage."

Brandon sat with Zach on the lone bench he had rested on previously. Staring at Zach's stricken profile, he couldn't imagine what his parents were discussing, but knew it wouldn't be good. Hannah was hiding behind a tree, staring at them.

Brandon shouted, "Get lost, you asshole!"

She would duck behind the trunk, then poke her head out again.

After what seemed like hours, Lois made her way over to them. "Come on, boys, we have to get to the airport."

Brandon nodded, standing up, reaching back to help Zach.

With an effort they got him to his feet. He wouldn't meet anyone's eye.

As they walked back to the hotel room, Brandon asked his mother quietly, "So? Are we dead?"

"We'll discuss it more when we get home."

At that direct comment, Brandon shut his mouth. *Yes, we're dead.*

The rest of the journey to the airport and home was completely silent. No one spoke. Zach had withdrawn into his own world, and Brandon wasn't even allowed to sit next to him on the plane or the drive home. It was the beginning of the end.

Chapter Thirteen

October 2005

Brandon Townsend sat at his computer in his office in Manhattan. He finished up his paragraph and hit the send button on the email, delivering the item to the magazine editing department.

"Mr. Townsend?"

Brandon looked up at the woman standing in his doorway.

"The car is waiting for you."

"Thanks, Melinda." He grabbed his briefcase, and overnight bag, shoved his tickets into his jacket pocket, and tossed his leather jacket over his arm.

"Have a nice trip, sir."

"Thanks. See you in a week." Stopping at the office next to his, he poked his head in and was disappointed to find it empty. He took the elevator to the ground floor and found a taxi parked out front. Tossing his briefcase into the back seat, handing his luggage to the driver to be stowed in the trunk, Brandon sat down behind the driver's seat and took out his mobile phone. As they headed to Kennedy Airport, Brandon's call connected, "Hey, Lori, I just checked your office and you were gone. I'm on my way to the airport now. Any last meaningful words of advice?"

"Oh, you outa here already?" she replied.

"Yeah. Already in the taxi."

"Have fun, cutie. Don't do anything I wouldn't do."

"That doesn't leave much, Ms. Mason."

"Ha, ha. You are a character, Mr. Townsend. What can I possibly tell you about the firm and the lawsuit that you don't already know?"

"I don't know. I'm just bored and looking for someone to chat to on the drive to the airport." He gazed wistfully out at the traffic as they drove through mid-town.

"Just don't get snowed in."

"Snowed in? It's the first week in October. Even Boston doesn't get snow that early."

"Don't be surprised."

"Crap, I hate flying. Always have."

"You could have driven. It's only five hours."

"Yeah, I should have. Would you have come with me?"

"No! You kidding? You know how much work I have to do while you're gone. Give me a break, Brandon. Someone's got to do all the shit-work with you out of the office for a week."

"Speaking of that, why the hell did Shelby make it a week? Can't I get to the bottom of this bullshit in a day?"

"You know, Shel. He wants the complete story. Besides, I've seen Melinda's list for you. It's going to take you a week to meet with all those contacts."

"Crap."

"Brandon…"

"Yeah?" He felt impatient as the cab stopped for a traffic light.

"Why don't you pursue your own writing career and quit this stupid magazine?"

Grinning, he replied, "I love you, you know that?"

She laughed. "If you weren't gay, I'd be excited."

"Oh? That means just because I'm gay I can't excite a woman?" Brandon noticed the taxi driver's eyes dart to the rearview mirror.

"Oh, no, good looking, you can excite a woman, believe me."

Smiling, Brandon sighed, "Okay, sweetie, let me go. I gotta get ready for this. The traffic's a mess and god knows what security is going to be like at the airport."

"Look, call me. You've got my mobile number. I don't care if you wake me up. If you get lonely in that hotel room of yours, we can always have phone sex."

"Yeah? How deep can you make your voice go?" he laughed, amused.

She tried to go a few octaves lower, "How about this?"

"Nice try. See ya."

"Bye!"

He hung up and pocketed his phone, feeling content, then caught the nasty look from the driver in the rearview mirror again and ignored it.

The one thing Brandon hated most about his current job was the traveling. He had a fantastic condo in Manhattan but was never home to enjoy it. Once again checking into a five star hotel, the weariness of the flight and cab rides already making him fatigued, he handed his business credit card to the clerk behind the desk and imagined a cognac and a snooze. He was given a key and went on his way.

Finally alone in the room, Brandon kicked off his shoes, called room service for his drink, and loosened his tie. Before he stripped off his suit he waited for that knock from room service on the door. After giving the man a tip and thanking him, Brandon took his glass, placing it on the nightstand. Once he undressed, he sat on the bed with the remote control in one hand and his drink in the other. He had an early start in the morning and knew he had to get a good night's rest.

His eyes growing heavy, the drink consumed, he shut off the TV and rolled against the pillows anticipating the wake up call and the work after it.

Chapter Fourteen

The cab dropped him off at a sleek steel-blue tinted glass skyscraper. Once Brandon handed the man the fare money, he stood tall on the cold, windy sidewalk, looking up at the impressive building. After stepping into the lobby, he tamed his windblown hair and pressed the button for the elevator. A smartly dressed woman stood next to him. He smiled politely at her.

They entered the elevator together and he asked her, "What floor do you need?"

"Seven, please."

He pushed the button for her.

After a brief moment of silence she asked, "Do you work in this building?"

"No. Just here for an appointment."

"Oh. Too bad." Digging through her purse, she handed him a business card, hissing seductively, "I'm Sharon Tice, call me."

Taking it politely, smiling to himself at the compliment, the elevator stopped at his floor. He whispered goodbye to her, then to his surprise he felt her squeeze his bottom before he stepped out. He spun back to look at her just as the doors began to close. A very wicked smirk appeared on the pretty woman's face. Standing there for a minute to compose himself after the bold caress to his derriere, he cleared his throat, straightened his tie, and made his way through the glass door to the receptionist.

"Yes, hello, my name is Brandon Townsend. I have an appointment with Mr. John Cade."

"Just one moment. Could you have a seat?" She gestured to a group of leather chairs near the door. He nodded and sat down, looking at a *People* magazine with little interest as it lay on a glass table top announcing the world's sexiest man. Glancing behind the receptionist, the firm's name was written in bold letters, *Cade, McMann, & Lucas Attorneys at Law.*

A moment later a stately older gentleman approached him, his hand held out in greeting. "Mr. Townsend, nice to meet you. Come in."

"Mr. Cade." Brandon returned his firm handshake. "It was really nice of you to allow me to come here for an interview."

"My pleasure. Come this way. I hope you don't mind my office."

"No. Not at all."

"Would you like a cup of coffee?"

"No. Thank you, sir." Brandon smiled politely, following the well-dressed man, gazing casually into the lush expensive offices as they passed. On each door was printed the name of an attorney. Out of the corner of his eye he spotted *Zachary E. Sherman*'s name written on a plaque.

As that name digested in his brain, he stopped short, backtracked, and stared at the name again. "Zachary?" he mumbled.

"Mr. Townsend?" Mr. Cade asked.

Seeing that name disoriented him. Brandon tried to convince himself it wasn't *his* Zachary. Not the Zachary who was torn away from him ten years ago. Not the Zachary who never again communicated with him when he was sent to college in another unknown state. Sent away without a goodbye. Was it that Zachary Sherman? The one who never once tried to contact him even though Brandon had stayed in New Jersey? Had gone to NYU and lived at home? That Zachary?

Moving past the empty room as if it were a train wreck, Brandon felt a sensation of nausea in his mid-section and wished he had a few moments to collect himself before he had to interview Mr. Cade. Entering the older man's office, sitting down, opening up his briefcase to get a notepad, Brandon remembered how many times he had tried to find Zach. Googled his name, begged Mr. or Mrs. Sherman for a hint, a clue. But they had stopped talking to anyone named Townsend after that fateful trip to Disney World. Best friends had turned to mortal enemies. So much so that after two years the Shermans moved. No forwarding address was left for even a Christmas card once a year. The severed friendship was so catastrophic it needed to be cauterized to stop the bleeding.

Was it his Zachary Emerson Sherman?

"Right…" Mr. Cade clasped his hands together on the desktop, as if waiting for an interrogation. "I suppose you want our point of view on the case? Oh, and no tape recorder, please. Just a notepad, if you don't mind."

Suddenly, Brandon could care less about politics, religion, or even the Great Pumpkin. He wanted to ask Mr. Cade if that man, *that man* in that office back there, was his man. And where was he? Was he married with children? Gay and out? Fat and bald?

Struggling to think, Brandon replied, "Yes. Of course. No. No recorder. Just this." He held up his pen and pad. "Since you represent the defendant, I would like any insight you could give me. I know, of course, you are limited by privilege…" Brandon was on autopilot. He couldn't care less about this case. But he was sent here to interview both sides in what his magazine considered a big news conflicting story, so here he was.

Mr. Cade gave him nothing of value. The double-talk and generalizations were something Brandon could have written in his office in Manhattan. But he didn't care anymore. Nodding, scribbling, giving small noises to encourage Mr. Cade to continue, all Brandon could think about was getting back to that other office and snooping around.

With the door to their room slightly ajar, Brandon heard a voice just outside. A shiver ran up his spine. "Excuse me, Mr. Cade. I'm sorry to interrupt you, but would you mind if I stopped here for a minute? I have to visit the men's room. It'll just be for a moment."

"No, of course not. Let me show you where it is."

They stood. Brandon nodded, gesturing for Mr. Cade to show him the way. As they walked though the hall, past that office once more, Brandon caught sight of a man's broad back, dark hair, and heard that deep resonating voice. He was speaking to a very attractive woman, who was smiling brightly.

Hoping it was his secretary and not his wife, Brandon was dying to see Zach's face. It had been ten years. And what a difference the time would make from seventeen to twenty-seven. Two questions were answered already. Not fat, not bald. And Brandon had known Zach would become as large and handsome as his father.

Brandon was shown the door to the men's room. "I'll meet you back at your office, sir. Just be a minute." Mr. Cade smiled, nodding.

Brandon entered the men's room, relieved himself, then washed his hands and stared at his reflection in the mirror. What would Zach think? Would he think he was as cute as he had been in high school? Would Zach run and jump into his arms? Or would he scowl at him and tell him to fuck off?

"Oh, Christ..." Brandon was so nervous his hands were damp and cold. "Don't get your hopes up, Brandy. He's most likely married with three kids." Standing straight, wishing himself luck, Brandon made his way back down that eternally long, lit corridor. When he came near to that open door with *Zachary E. Sherman* emblazoned on it, he paused, listening like a good nosy journalist should.

The woman was overtly flirting. A tittering laugh and purring compliment; Brandon was about to barf. Finally, the twit moved closer to the door, as if making her exit. Brandon could actually hear her words now.

"Yes…I will, Zach. No problem. Right away. Uh huh. You bet." When she stepped out in the hall she inhaled a breath in surprise. "Can I help you?"

"No. I just need to see Mr. Sherman."

"Is he expecting you?"

"I doubt that very much." Brandon couldn't help but smile.

Inside the office, Zach heard his secretary asking someone in the hall questions. Tilting his head, he was about to see what was going on when a fantastic looking man in a silky designer business suit turned the corner and stood in his doorway. Knowing exactly who it was, but astonished to see him there, Zach choked.

Once Zach's secretary left, Brandon stepped into his office, smiled and whispered, "Hello, Mr. Sherman."

Gaping in awe, Zach said, "Brandon? What the hell?"

Brandon looked down the hall first, then whispered, "I'm interviewing Cade. Are you going to be here for a bit?"

Nodding, his mouth hanging open, Zach didn't answer verbally.

"Good. Wait for me. I'm wrapping it up now."

When he left, Zach dropped down on his chair to get over the shock. Never in a million years had he ever expected to see that man again. The chastising over their relationship hit so deep, was so brutal, Zach promised himself he would never suffer that humiliation again. His mother's voice resounded in his head. *It's just a stage you're going through, it will pass. You will eventually find women are right for you. This thing with*

Brandon was just something young boys sometimes did. Nothing to worry about. Forget it ever happened. Just put him out of your mind and go live with Uncle David and get your education. Law? Of course you can study law. Anything you want, Zachary. Just move to Boston, live with Uncle David, and never contact that troubled young man again. If you do as we say, we'll pay for your degree. You got that, Zach? If you don't, well, you don't want to know what'll happen if you try to see him. Go find a nice woman. Settle down. Have children. No one ever has to know about this silly little phase you went through. It's finished. Now you can be a real man.

Be a real man.

He was a real man, wasn't he? And after seeing Brandon, he was hard as a rock.

Brandon was lost in his thoughts, his memories. Nodding, knowing nothing this senior partner was saying was sinking in, he made the moves of someone who was trying to escape. "Yes. I do understand your point of view. I do. I'll interview the other partners of course. No, I respect that. I do." Brandon was about to chew off his foot to get out of the trap that the claustrophobic office had become. Zach was waiting. Zach. The man he never stopped pining over once he'd lost him. That man.

Standing, reaching over the desk, Brandon shook Mr. Cade's hand. "I can show myself out. Thank you so much for your time, sir."

"I do hope you won't slant the article against us, Mr. Townsend. As you can see, bad publicity of any kind for a law firm can be quite damaging."

"It's not our policy to slander, Mr. Cade. Please, have no fear on that account."

"Thank you, son. I appreciate that."

Nodding, Brandon tried not to race out of Mr. Cade's office and down the hall. When he finally did get free of the confines of that room, he had to force himself not to sprint to Zach like he was sixteen and running next door.

Seeing Zach sitting in his chair behind an impressive desk, Brandon smiled proudly at him and what he had accomplished. Stepping inside, smelling Zach's tantalizing cologne, Brandon whispered, "Hello, again."

Having the time to recuperate from the shock, Zach asked, "What the hell brought you here? How did you manage to find me?" Zach stood, moved to the door, looked out in paranoia and shut it. As if this were a clandestine meeting, he drew the curtains over the glass panes giving them complete privacy.

"No. It wasn't you that brought me here. I had an assignment to interview three members of your law firm on that bankruptcy case."

"Oh." Zach appeared slightly disappointed the search wasn't to find him. "Christ, Brandy, it's been so long."

"Ten long, mother-fucking years, Zach." Brandon set his briefcase down on the floor near a chair. "I'm afraid to even ask. I know you must be married."

Zach held out his hands, showing no ring. "Going through a divorce at the moment."

"Any kids?"

"No, thank fuck."

"When did you get married?"

"First year of law school. It was the biggest mistake of my life."

"The biggest?" Brandon asked, tilting his head.

A deep breath came out of Zach's chest. "Oh, Brandy, look at you. You are so fucking good looking."

"And out."

"Sorry?" Zach questioned.

"I'm out, Zach."

"No shit?"

"No shit."

"Uh, out and have a partner?"

"No. Out and don't have a partner."

"Oh?"

Brandon sank down heavily on the chair. "Why didn't you contact me? Do you have any idea how much I cried? Looked for you? Begged your parents to give me a clue where you were?"

Zach's face dropped as if guilt had found its way to his somber mood. Sitting on the desk in front of Brandon, Zach replied, "I know."

Waiting, Brandon threw up his hands in exasperation. "That's it? You know?"

Zach rubbed his eyes tiredly.

"After everything we'd been through? Did together? All I get after ten years is, 'I know'?"

"Look, Brandy…"

A rap at the door interrupted them. Zach stood off the desk, crossed the room, and opened it. That pretty secretary was there, trying to see inside as if she were the jealous, soon to be ex-spouse. "Here's the file you needed."

"Thanks." Zach took it.

"You going to lunch soon?"

"No. I'm busy." Zach closed the door on her pout, threw the file on his desk, and sat back down on it again.

Brandon waited, bristling with jealousy. "Screwed her, didn't you? Is that why you're divorcing? Cheated on the wife?"

"Forget her. Look, Brandy, it was a phase. All right? Just something guys do when their hormones are raging."

In anger, Brandon stood. "You know who you sound like?" Zach didn't answer. "Your homophobic father. Sorry I bothered you." Brandon made a move to the door. When he felt Zach's hand on his arm, he froze. The memories flooded back to him with so much clarity, he felt a lump come to his throat.

"Brandy…"

Brandon thought sadly, *No one has called me that in a decade.* And he missed it. Biting down his emotions, he bravely turned to face Zach. "Fine, Zach. It was some stupid adolescent phase. Fine. Look. I have two more interviews to do in this office, then I'll be gone."

"Are you still living in Jersey?"

"No. New York."

"Did you end up going to NYU?" Zach didn't let go of Brandon's arm.

"Yeah, believe it? That's where you were meant to go."

"I ended up at Northeastern. Then got my law degree at Boston U."

Brandon shrugged. "Gee, thanks for telling me, Zach."

"I was living with my Uncle David. He kept a tight leash on me, Brandon. You have no idea."

"Oh, come on!" Brandon shook off the hold Zach had on his forearm. "You couldn't make one fricken phone call? Write one letter? I lived at home. I never moved out. I commuted for four years. You're the one who disappeared, not me!"

Zach turned away and sat in the leather chair behind his desk, his eyes glazed and staring out at the Boston skyline.

Brandon tried to relax his tightly wound back muscles. He hadn't even realized he was tensing them. Dropping down in the chair again, he leaned on Zach's desk and stared at him for a long, silent moment, then in a hoarse whisper, he said, "Christ, you look fantastic, Zachary. I can't believe it. Better looking than your dad."

A soft chuckle came out of Zach's throat. "Dad died, Brandon."

Stunned, Brandon sat up. "No! When?"

"He was coming home late from work one night. Fell asleep at the wheel and wrapped himself around a guardrail."

"Oh, Christ, Zach..." Brandon felt sick.

"Yeah, two years ago."

Brandon moved instinctively to be near him. Standing beside his chair, Brandon touched Zach's shoulder gently. "I'm so sorry, Zach. How did Maude take it?"

"She died that day with him, but her body doesn't know it. She's walking around like a fucking wraith."

"Oh, baby..." Brandon brushed his fingers through Zach's thick dark hair.

"Hannah freaked out. She had to go for therapy. Still is."

"Zach, I wish I could have been there for you." He petted Zach's hair back, loving its full, thick softness. When Zach wrapped around Brandon's waist for an embrace, Brandon closed his eyes. The relief of having this man in his life again was finally sinking in. "I don't know what to say. I just wish I had known."

Zach inhaled Brandon's scent. That familiar masculine aroma of his skin, felt his body heat, remembered the first time they had played, *I'll show you mine if you show me yours*, in his closet with flashlights. Remembered their first kiss in the built-in pool in his house in Fair Lawn at midnight, the discovery of anal sex in Zelene's parents' bedroom, of the fateful trip to Florida when everything fell apart. It all swept back to him like a dream. And ever since that time, Zach hadn't had the treat of male flesh. Just women. Too many women to count, and one that he considered his biggest mistake: his current soon-to-be-ex-wife. The experience left him cold. He married so he could show his old man he wasn't queer. Well? After ten years of seeing a therapist to get his head straight Zach asked himself, "Now what?"

The Boy Next Door

When Brandon felt Zach touching the front of his pants, he looked down quickly. "What are you doing, Zach?"

"Nothing, Brandy."

Brandon stepped back. Zach dropped his hands and looked up innocently at him.

Crossing his arms over his chest, Brandon warned, "What is this? Some sentimental gesture on your part? Making up for ten lost years?"

"No. I'm sorry, Brandon."

"I was just some stupid phase, right? Some stupid mistake you made when your hormones were racing?"

"Brandon, please."

Another rap rattled the door. That secretary again. "Zach? Court in ten minutes!"

"Shit," Zach mumbled. Then he shouted, "Okay." Standing up, looking around in distraction, it appeared to Brandon that Zach was completely flummoxed.

What was Brandon supposed to do? The damage Zach had done to his heart was so deep, so lethal... Was he supposed to just pretend it hadn't happen?

Zach found his paperwork and put it into his briefcase. "Where are you staying, Brandon?"

"Why?"

"I thought we could meet for dinner and catch up. I don't even know what you've been doing for the last decade."

"No. How unfortunate for you that you didn't call me to find out."

"Brandy...please..." Zach begged, "Try to understand."

"Try to understand? Oh, you have to be kidding."

Zach lowered his head, moving to the door.

With a sigh, Brandon whispered, "Radisson. Near the waterfront."

Smiling adorningly at him, Zach nodded, then left.

Brandon could see that pointy-faced blonde waiting for him giving him the evil eye for taking Zach's precious time away from her. Oh, Zach screwed her all right. "Something we have in common!" he felt like shouting down the hall to her. When the anger began to seep out, pain took its place. On his walk down the hall to his next appointment, all Brandon could do was ask himself why. Why did it take this chance meeting for them to find each other? Why? Why didn't Zach write, call, email, get in touch with him? Why? And until he got a better answer than *he thought the gay thing was a phase*, he couldn't forgive.

Chapter Fifteen

Sitting in the lounge at the hotel, Brandon sipped a cocktail and heard his mobile phone ringing. Taking it out of his suit jacket pocket, he read the display, answering it. "Hey, Lori."

"Hey, surgarplum. How did the interviews go?"

"Waste of time. Three old men telling me nothing I didn't know already."

"You sound like shit. Was it that bad?"

Sighing, looking at the few tipsy patrons that were scattered around the dimly lit bar, Brandon replied, "Ran into an old flame."

"Oh? I take it it's not a happy reunion."

"Yes and no. I can't really get into it right now. Too many Bush-supporters stinking of bourbon and reminiscing about the good ol' days."

"Where are you?"

"Drowning my sorrows in the hotel lounge."

"Poor baby."

"How was your day, Lori?" Brandon nodded to the bartender to get him a refill.

"Finished the Christmas issue's commentary on the lousy events of last year."

"Oh, what fun..." Brandon whispered thank you to the

bartender as he set down a fresh drink.

A pause followed, then Lori asked, "How did your old flame end up in Boston?"

"Long story. Let's just say, he was the adorable boy next door and we used to play doctor together." He took the umbrella out of the fresh Tequila Sunrise and set it into his empty glass.

"Married with two point four kids?"

"No. Divorcing with zero offspring. But he's blatantly decided to be hetero." Brandon peeked at another old man who plopped down right next to him, smelling of stale dust or mothballs. Turning his back to the man, Brandon sighed, "Christ, I feel like I'm at a World War II veteran's convention."

Lori burst out laughing. "I love you, you know that?"

"Stop. I'm blushing." Brandon looked back at the old man who ordered a shot of something brown. "Look, let me suck down my pretty orange cocktail and lick my wounds."

"Okay. Remember, I'm here if you need a shoulder to cry on."

"Thanks, darling. See ya." Brandon hung up, slipped the phone into his pocket and sipped his drink, staring at the television that had CNN on with closed captions running a commentary under the talking heads.

Zach pulled his jacket collar up higher against the wind. Craning his neck at the tower of the Radisson's hotel block, he figured it had to be the correct one since he knew of no other that close to the waterfront. On the drive over, all he kept mumbling over and over again was, "Brandy, Brandy, Brandy."

"You were supposed to stay hidden, Brandon. A page in my life history that was torn out and shredded. How on earth could fate turn you up at my office door?" Zach cursed it at the same time he thanked god. But in reality, he was so confused he didn't know what to think. The trauma that had accompanied the discovery of their little teenage fling was so long lasting,

Zach promised himself he'd follow the straight and narrow, with the emphasis on straight. Why had Brandon shown up? Why did he look so fucking amazing? And why was he openly gay?

Why, why, why?

And why was Zach standing in the hotel lobby, looking for him? Looking for trouble? Looking for anal sex? Looking for what?

His mobile phone rang just as he stepped into the warm crystal and glass covered lobby. Moving back to the window with its dark view of streetlights and traffic, Zach took it out of his coat pocket. "Hello."

"Zachy-baby, where are you?"

Cringing, Zach wasn't even divorced yet and another woman had already dug in her claws. "Jillian, I'm busy."

"You're not with *her*, are you?"

The jealous reference to his soon to be ex-wife curdling his blood, Zach sighed in exhaustion. "I still live with 'her', remember? But, no. I'm meeting with a friend. Okay?"

"What friend? A male friend?"

The possessiveness was already getting on his nerves. What was it about women that they needed…and needed…and needed, until he felt sucked dry? "Please, give me a break, Jillian."

"When will you come to my place? Can you call me later?"

Grinding his teeth in frustration, he said, "No. Let me go." He hung up before he heard another comment. He wondered if she would now sue him for sexual harassment since she was his legal secretary, after all. He shut off the phone so he didn't have to deal with her or his wife again for the night.

His attention back on the front desk, Zach made his way over and waited his turn as an old man checked in and couldn't seem to find his credit card. After shifting from leg to leg impatiently, Zach finally got to ask the clerk, "Yes, I'm looking for Brandon Townsend. He's staying here."

"Do you know his room number?"

"No." Zach leaned on the desk, feeling overheated in the warm lobby.

"Yes, he is. Would you like me to ring his room?"

"Please." Zach felt relieved, checked his watch, noticed it was nearing seven and wondered what Brandon was doing.

The man hung up the phone. "There's no answer in his room. Would you like me to leave a message?"

Zach's heart sank. Trying to decide if he should leave a message, admit he was indeed there looking for that openly gay man, he was about to say no, when he noticed several aging codgers making their way into a dimly lit lounge. "That the bar?" Zach pointed at it.

"Yes, sir. Our cocktail lounge and restaurant. Would you like me to see if Mr. Townsend is inside?"

As hope sparked again in him, Zach shook his head. "No. But I wouldn't mind having a look myself."

"Certainly, sir."

Zach removed his wool coat, tucked it over his arm, then ran his hand through his hair as he entered the area of poor lighting and candle-lit tables.

Brandon tipped the last sip of his third cocktail down his throat. Imagining a late dinner and then some work on the laptop before bed, he dug in his pocket and tossed a few bills on the counter. Standing, checking he had everything he needed, he spun around, intending on making his way to the restaurant when he noticed someone standing at the entrance of the bar looking in. "Oh, I don't believe it."

Zach found him in the crowded room. Their gazes locked.

Wondering what Zach intended to do once they met up

again, Brandon closed the gap between them and stared into those sky blue eyes. "What do you want?"

Zach's face soured as if he expected a more excited greeting. "Just to talk."

"I was about to go to the restaurant and eat dinner."

"Mind some company?"

Brandon thought that comment over carefully. He did mind, but in reality he couldn't imagine telling Zach to leave. "No." Leading the way to the host and the entrance of the restaurant, Brandon asked for a table for two. They were silently shown to a private, candle-lit spot.

Zach draped his coat over the back of the chair and sat down. Brandon couldn't get over how fit Zach was and tried not to let the desire to see him naked color his attitude on the treatment he had received in the past.

Once they were both comfortable and leaning their elbows on the table, staring at each other, Brandon wondered if their meeting could get any more awkward. "Christ, Zach, say something. You look like a fucking zombie."

Shaking himself out of the trance, Zach picked up the menu and stared at it instead.

Brandon sighed tiredly, decided on a meal quickly, laid the menu down, and looked around for the waiter to come and end the fiasco of their unhappy reunion.

When the waiter showed up with his pad and pen, Brandon ordered a seafood salad while Zach asked for meat. A bottle of wine was brought to the table at Zach's request. Brandon wondered bitterly if this was how he wooed the women in his life.

Finally left alone, the wine glasses full, the candle flickering in an unseen breeze, Brandon sipped the red liquid for lack of anything better to do. In exasperation, he growled, "Zachary! Either say something or get the fuck out of here. I don't need a mannequin to keep me company."

"I'm sorry."

Brandon glared at him. "Is that an 'I'm sorry for being a mannequin' or 'I'm sorry for ignoring you for ten years'?" When nothing verbal was offered in answer, Brandon looked more closely at Zachary's face. It appeared as if Zach was battling back his emotions. Brandon began to feel guilty, though in some part of his brain he thought, "Good, cry! I did for a decade!"

After what appeared to be a considerable effort on Zach's part to be able to open his lips and say a few words, he whispered, "Sorry for the ten years."

Leaning as close as he could across that tiny table and lit flame, Brandon demanded, "Why didn't you call me? Huh? Why? Zach, the last time we talked or saw each other was on the damn drive home from the airport after Orlando. What the hell happened to you to forget I existed?" Brandon tried to lower his voice. "I couldn't figure it out. I died every day. The rejection you put me through killed me. Do you have any idea how long it took for me to date someone? To try and have a social life?"

"You...you dated guys?"

Brandon threw up his hands in exasperation. Holding back his rage, Brandon hissed, "Yes! Okay? Yes, I date guys. Did I fall in love? No! Ask me why I never fell in love, Zachary!"

A single tear slipped down Zach's high cheekbone. Zach quickly wiped it dry.

Brandon took a few deep breaths to calm down. "Please..." Brandon begged, "I need one good reason why you never tried. Please."

Zach was fighting so hard not to cry, he was in pain. Biting his lip, wringing his hands, shifting his legs, shuffling his feet, he was about to excuse himself to sob alone where no one could stare. But he didn't. Holding on to that last string of self-control, he swallowed the lump in his throat and managed to get out, "I loved you too much."

Brandon tilted his head in confusion.

Peering around their table at the other diners first, Zach cleared his throat, trying to get his vocal cords to cooperate, and repeated, "I...I loved you too much, Brandy. I was petrified of that love."

"Why?" Brandon whined softly.

Fidgeting again, cursing himself for being so weak, Zach scanned the area to see if anyone was staring at the sad case of quivering masculinity he'd become. "I...I didn't want to be labeled a queer."

It appeared Brandon was about to explode.

"Brandy," Zach implored, "try to understand. Please."

"Oh, I do, Zach, make no mistake."

By Brandon's tone, Zach knew it was a losing battle. So much had happened to him after he arrived in Boston, he didn't know where to begin. "You were always better with words than I was."

"Bullshit," Brandon scoffed. "It was math I was better at. You're the one who became a goddamn lawyer."

"Yeah, but you're the goddamn journalist." When Brandon's face lost some of its rage, Zach felt a sense of relief. "Look, Brandon, I did what thousands of other guys do. I hid my true feelings. The amount of pressure I felt from my parents to go off and become this image of a man they had always had in their head was like an anvil around my neck."

"When you left for Boston, the noose of Sly Sherman was cut," Brandon sneered, his top lip curling, revealing his perfect white teeth.

Before Zach could defend himself, their food arrived. Hating the pause between that comment and his excuse, Zach waited impatiently for the waiter to move on. When he did, Zach stared at his food with little interest.

Brandon began eating.

Zach picked up his fork but didn't touch his plate. "Brandon, Uncle David was worse than Dad."

"Yeah, huh," Brandon replied in disbelief.

"He monitored my calls. He picked me up after class. He had spies watching my every move."

"Oh, shut the fuck up," Brandon scoffed.

Zach held back another emotional outburst, tried to calm himself, and with a supreme effort, he whispered, "He beat the fuck out of me, Brandon."

Brandon stopped eating and stared at him.

Zach looked around once more, leaning across the candle flame. "The first day I arrived in Boston... Dad drove me there himself. He and Uncle David had a long talk in another room. When they came out, David and Dad used me like a punching bag. They kept shouting they would beat the gay out of me."

Brandon set his fork down, his eyes glistening.

"I had a month to heal before I started college, Brandon. I was so bruised I couldn't look at myself in the mirror. David warned me if he even suspected I tried to contact you, he'd put me in the hospital." Zach swallowed down the painful memory. "And he did, Brandy. I was on the phone in my room, talking to a classmate. David picked up the extension like he did each time I made a call. I have no idea why, but he thought I was talking to you. He didn't even wait to ask. He barged into the bedroom, grabbed me by the throat and broke my jaw he hit me so hard."

Brandon's eyes widened, his stare never wavering.

Lowering his gaze, Zach cleared his throat and waited for the information to digest. After a minute, he continued, "I couldn't take the chance, Brandon. The first two years were the worst. Then, just to get everyone off my back, I dated some stupid girl. I made a point of bringing her to Uncle David's house as much as I could. I kissed her in front of him, did things to make him believe that I was 'cured'. I couldn't take another beating, Brandy. My jaw was wired for weeks after what he did."

"Why didn't you go to the cops?"

Smiling sadly, Zach whispered, "Uncle David was a prosecutor, you're kidding, right?"

The waiter stood over them and asked, "Is the meal all right?"

Brandon smiled at him, saying, "Yes. Thank you."

Zach waited for him to leave, then sat back, staring at Brandon.

Brandon felt so sick to his stomach from the conversation, he lost his appetite. Rubbing his face in anguish, he finally looked back at those punished blue eyes and said, "I had no idea."

"How could you? It wasn't like I could call you and tell you."

"Oh, Zach, I'm so angry about it. I swear I could kill someone."

"Believe me, that thought crossed my mind. Look, Brandon, you have to realize being straight became the path of least resistance. Going to school, still dependant on those bastards, I couldn't afford to move out, and they refused to pay for the dorm. It wasn't until I graduated, passed the BAR, and began earning money that I was able to get out from under their clutches. And by then, I met Brook and married her. Again, it seemed like what I was supposed to do. She was working for another law firm, we got along okay, and everyone was off my back.

"And it had been years, Brandon. By then I imagined you were either married as well, or involved with another guy and not interested in me any longer. I mean, how long did I expect you to wait for me? I knew what you must have thought. I knew you thought I deserted you, that I somehow got you out of my blood and brain and moved on. I never did, Brandy. I never did." Wiping at his eyes again, he whispered, "Brandy, I was in counseling for almost a decade. After what dad and Uncle David did to me, I was a wreck. At least with Dr. Morris, I could tell him my real feelings. He knew I was gay and hiding. But just because I could tell my shrink the truth didn't mean I could come out, wave a rainbow flag, and announce what I really was. I was so petrified after what I had been through, I thought even if a hint of gayness came out of me, someone somewhere would kick my ass."

Brandon watched as Zach dabbed at his tears again. Instinctively, Brandon moved his leg under the table to contact Zach. And in response to that touch, Zach's leg pressed back against his.

"You..." Zach choked back his sobs, "You were my dream. My boy next door. Oh, Christ, Brandy, how on earth did I ever know I'd meet my soul-mate at two years old."

"One. We met at one." Brandon smiled sweetly.

"Knowing our moms, it was most likely even before that." Zach kept wiping at his eyes.

Brandon couldn't believe everything he was hearing. Well, it certainly was better than the excuse of "it was just a phase". But it was very painful to learn.

Zach finally took a bite of his meal. After he chewed, he sipped his wine. "How on earth did your parents deal with the fallout after Florida?"

Sighing heavily, Brandon picked up his fork but didn't eat. "Polar opposites to what you dealt with, Zach."

"Really? Even from Mel?"

"Yup, even from my dad. We had a long family discussion about it, Zach. The day after we got home from Orlando, the three of us sat in the living room and talked for hours."

"You're telling me, your dad, Mel Townsend, accepted

you for being gay?"

Seeing the disbelief on Zach's face, Brandon felt guilty he had it so easy. "Yes. My dad accepted it."

Zach sat back in his chair, a look of complete awe on his face.

Shrugging, Brandon said, "I don't know why, Zach. He just didn't have the hang-ups your dad did. But my dad had another son. Reece married and has three kids. Maybe that made it easier for me."

"I don't believe it. I imagined you'd be put through the same thing as I was. It was another reason I was petrified to contact you. I figured if your dad found a letter from me, he'd beat the crap out of you."

"No." Brandon shook his head to emphasize it. "I'm telling you, Zach, he was cool."

When Zach put his fork down and covered his face again, Brandon whispered, "Zach, let's get out of here. Neither of us is eating."

Lowering his hands, Zach nodded. "I should let you go."

"What?" Brandon asked in anger. "Go?"

Zach sat upright and replied, "Isn't that what you meant?"

"No, you dork! Come to my room where we can talk more privately." Brandon waved at the waiter. When he approached their table and found two uneaten meals he seemed upset. "Can we have the check, please?" Brandon asked.

"Do you want me to box these up?"

"No. It wasn't bad food. Believe me." Brandon tried to reassure him.

The waiter nodded and went to get their check. When Brandon looked across the table, he found Zach's exhausted smile.

They were standing at Brandon's door a few minutes later.

Brandon opened it and stepped in, seeing the bed made and new towels in the bath. He tossed the key on the dresser, loosening his tie as he walked across the room. Behind him, Zach closed and locked the door, then dropped his coat on a chair.

Shaking his head, Brandon laughed. "Wow. You and me in a hotel room. I don't know whether to jump for joy or shiver at the bad memories."

"Me neither, Brandy. Me neither."

"Take off your tie. Relax. You don't have to get home right away, do you?"

"No. I don't have to get home." Zach opened the knot of his tie and slid it out of his collar.

Brandon sat on the bed comfortably. "So, tell me about this divorce. What stage are you at?"

"Negotiation. She's trying to bankrupt me." Removing his suit jacket, Zach tossed it over his wool coat on the chair, then lay his tie down on top of the pile. Once he had kicked off his shoes he sat next to Brandon on the bed, reclining back on it. "I cheated on her. She went ballistic."

"With that bimbo in your office?"

"Yeah. How'd you guess?"

"I could see how possessive she was. Man, you sure know how to pick them." Brandon stretched out next to Zach on the bedspread.

"My choices suck, Brandy. Believe me. It's another thing I've been in therapy for. Dr. Morris thinks I'm going crazy trying to prove something with women. He told me it wouldn't work. He's right, Brandy. I'm gay, period. I just haven't been able to face it yet. Maybe I can now." Zach opened the top buttons of his shirt to get comfortable.

"Look, Zach, don't keep blaming yourself. If I were beaten up the way you were, I'd be in therapy and pretending to be straight as well."

Zach moved closer, as if he needed to whisper. "What kind

of relationships have you had?"

Brandon smiled sadly. "Male ones."

"I know," Zach replied, looking more like his old self. "Tell me about them."

"Perv." Brandon grinned wickedly.

"You suck cock?"

"Yes..."

"We never got that far," Zach mused out loud. "Close but not quite." After a pause, he asked, "Did you like it?"

"Oh, yes." Brandon nodded. "I liked it a lot."

"You always use protection?"

Brandon's smile faded. "What's that supposed to mean?"

"Nothing." Zach raised his hands in defense.

"Do I have AIDS? Is that your next question?" Brandon shouted. "My guess is that you're the whore, not me."

"Brandy, calm down."

"Did I use protection..." Brandon fumed, mumbling under his breath.

Zach hissed, "Brandy...calm down." His hot hand found its way to Brandon's thigh.

Brandon looked down at it timidly. Was this going to happen? Was he ready for this? "What are you doing, Zach?"

"Stop asking me that question, Brandy."

"No. I won't stop asking it. Look, even though I do understand what happened to you. You know, why you couldn't contact me, et cetera, et cetera..." The hand grew slightly bolder. Brandon jumped as it did. "I...I live in New York, Zach. You live in Boston. I have a life there, you have a life here..." Those large fingers crawled slowly up Brandon's thigh headed to his crotch. "My heart can't take a tease, Zach. I can't let you come into my life, then suddenly you're mister heterosexual again, swapping spit with the blonde bimbo and the next minute you're humping me…"

"Shut up and kiss me."

Brandon's heart moved to his throat. Zach's lips were right there. Certainly near enough to kiss. Those male fingers crept closer to the hard mound in his pants. "Zach, please wait. I need to know what the hell this means first."

"It means I miss you. It means I need to touch you, Brandon."

"You? You, you, you?" Brandon inched his hips back as Zach rubbed his index finger over the flap of his zipper.

"What do you want, Brandy?"

At that seductive tone, Brandon melted. "What do I want? Will it mean anything to you? Make a difference to you?"

"Yes."

After swallowing down the intimidation of actually admitting what he truly wanted, he replied, "Something solid. I want a relationship that's committed. Not one that my other half needs to cheat, go out on me…"

Zach reacted to the insult, moving back on the bed so he could see Brandon's eyes more clearly. "That's not fair, Brandon. I told you what happened in my therapy sessions. It was just some denial thing I was going through."

"Was it? Do I know who the hell you are now? After ten years you've stuck your dick in pussy and I'm supposed to know who the hell you are?"

"Hey!"

Brandon hated himself for it, but it was reality. Was this his Zach? His affectionate boy next door? Or was he some lousy womanizer?

"What the hell did you say that for? Brandon, I was totally honest with you down there in the restaurant."

"Yes. I know." Brandon felt indignant suddenly. "You told me you're divorcing your wife because you can't keep your dick in your pants. And for some reason, it likes cunt now."

"Christ, Brandon!" Zach moved off the bed in anger, standing up, staring down at him. "No need to be crass!"

Brandon didn't know why he said those things. What he really wanted was to screw Zach's brains out. But how could he? So much had happened from then to now. He needed trust. He needed commitment. He needed stability. He'd been so trampled, he never thought he could love again. That feeling of bland numbness permeated every encounter he had. Each time a male suitor tried to climb that wall, Brandon shoved him back and never called him again. Love brought pain. Love brought isolation. No thank you.

"You want me to leave?" Zach reached for his jacket.

Just as Zach slid his arm into the sleeve of his garment, Brandon whispered, "No. Stay."

Obeying, Zach set his suit jacket back on the chair, standing still.

"Come back on the bed." Brandon patted the spot next to him.

Zach stretched out along side him, propping his head up on his palm.

Timidly, Brandon used his index finger to touch Zach's face. Starting at his forehead, he lightly drew a line across his dark eyebrow, then down his temple to his cheekbone. Brandon licked his lip unconsciously as he wove his finger down Zach's cheek to his mouth. Gently, Brandon stroked Zach's top lip, then his bottom, feeling the rough stubble on Zach's square jaw. He was lost on him. Brandon had tried to imagine what Zachary would look like as a full-grown man and never quite could. It was always tainted by the image of Sly, his father. But Zachary had far exceeded his father in the looks category. Those long black lashes framed the lightest of blue eyes. "Zach…" Brandon whispered, about to ask him something.

Zachary never waited to see what that question was. Rolling his weight on top of Brandon, pinning him to the bed under him, Zach went for those lips. On contact the memory of the first time they had kissed, standing in his parents' swimming pool at midnight, washed over him like a crashing tide. With his eyes closed, he envisioned the seventeen-year-old Brandon Townsend, beautiful, lithe, and androgynous. When he opened his eyes he found the adult version of the Ganymede he had fallen head over heels in love with. Brandon's eyes were closed tightly, his brows furrowed in pleasure.

Zach knew he could go mad over him. Knew he would tear off that fine silk suit just to feel the velvety softness of Brandon's skin. Sucking at Brandon's mouth, dueling tongues, licking at his teeth and wanting Brandon so much he could die, Zach knew this was where he needed to be. Life didn't have to be a mystery. Thousands of dollars in counseling sessions. In his arms he had the answer.

Brandon thought he was dreaming. Big, muscular, Zachary Sherman was writhing on him. His hard cock was rubbing against his own with an urgency that was too loud to ignore. The battle in his head being fought, his common sense telling him not to let go, not to trust in a man with a history of heterosexual infidelity, while the opposing side screamed for the naked contact of his flesh.

Breaking the kiss, panting for air, Brandon stared into those blue eyes. "Christ, Zach. It's as if we never parted."

"I know. I can't believe how much I've missed you. I feel sick about it."

Brandon tentatively reached down Zach's side, cupping his bottom tightly in his palm. "Nice ass, Zachary Emerson Sherman."

"You want it?" Zach's light eye blazed with fire.

"Ya got baby oil?"

Zach rolled onto his back at the hilarity, roaring with laughter, as Brandon did the same. It felt so good to laugh, Brandon let it out, tears streaming down his face. Gasping for breath as they contained their hysteria, Brandon wiped at his eyes and then twisted over to face Zach, his smile dropping to a serious expression. Brandon reached into Zach's trousers, the way Zach used to do to him while they were studying in Zach's bedroom. When Brandon felt the size and hardness of Zach's cock, he closed his eyes. "Oh, Jesus, Zachary. When the hell did you get so fucking huge?"

"I don't know. Somewhere between seventeen and twenty-seven I guess."

Brandon slipped his hand out so he could kneel on the bed, opening the belt, button, and zipper of Zach's dress slacks. Spreading wide the fabric, reaching into the dark blue briefs, Brandon exposed Zach's cock to admire. "Fucking beautiful."

"Yeah?" Zach craned his neck from off the pillow to look.

"Yeah." Brandon licked his lips. "Ah, you want a blow job?"

"Oh, fuck yeah!" Zachary yanked down his slacks, kicking them off the bed, opening his shirt.

Moving off the bed, Brandon did the same, staring down at Zachary's nakedness as his clothing vanished quickly. Brandon was slow to catch up, distracted by Zach's muscular frame. "Oh, Zach, I knew you would be fantastic. I knew it."

"Christ, look who's talking, Brandy." Zach grabbed his own cock and jerked it a few times as if he couldn't wait.

Dropping his last article of clothing onto the floor, Brandon knelt up on the bed and stared down at Zach's entire body, from head to toe. "Zachary...what can I say? You're exquisite."

"I'm gonna spurt, Brandy..." Zach rolled his hips anxiously from side to side. "Looking at you is such a fucking turn on."

"Better than a blonde cunt?"

"Shut up and get over here." Zach reached out hungrily.

Taking his time, not knowing if this fling was the prelude to a happily ever after relationship or a one time affair, Brandon smoothed his hand over Zachary's large thigh muscle. It was warm and tight and felt like concrete. "Oh, Christ..." Brandon whimpered, in longing. Maneuvering himself to crouch between those large thighs, Brandon pushed Zach's legs to a wide straddle. "*Oh...*" Brandon moaned at the view, knowing Zach was craving satisfaction.

"Brandy...I'm going nuts."

"I know. Oh, Zachary Sherman...look at your balls." Brandon shook his head, licking his lips. "I can't wait to suck on them like candy."

A low, deep moan emerged from Zach's chest. He spread his legs wider, reaching his hands down, begging.

Brandon lowered himself to be able to take those delicate balls into his mouth. Raising them up in his hand gently, he sucked on the right one, rolling his tongue over it in ecstasy. Zach whimpered and tensed his legs.

Next to devour was the left testicle. Sucking it into his hot mouth, Brandon closed his eyes and savored the taste, the feel of the tender tissue on his tongue. With his right index finger he stroked Zach, pushing the tip of his finger into his anus. Zach grunted in longing and gripped the bedspread under him with white knuckles.

Licking his way up to Zach's shaft, Brandon lapped at the base, wrapping his tongue around it like a snake. Raising up on his elbows, he traced the length with the tip of his tongue, causing Zach to quiver and moan. Showing off, for he knew damn well he gave better head than any female Zach would ever have encountered, Brandon took his time, licking that hard cock in pleasure.

"Brandy...make me come. Make me come," Zach pleaded.

Brandon could only smile demonically and slow down even more for some delicious sexual torment. Holding the base in his right hand, Brandon finally put the tip of Zach's cock in his mouth, instantly removing it, lapping at the soft ridge underneath. When he did it again, Brandon tasted the pre-come drop on his tongue. Smiling in pleasure, Brandon leaned up higher and plunged Zach's entire cock into his mouth. Zach shouted out in reflex and panted heavily. Sucking, swirling his tongue up and down the underside of the head of Zach's cock, Brandon knew it was a matter of seconds now. Fondling those balls, pushing into Zach's ass, Brandon sucked as hard and as fast as he could.

Zach felt he was convulsing the climax was so strong. Clenching every muscle in his body, he shot out come into Brandon's mouth and gasped in ecstasy. As he vocalized what was quite possibly the most intense orgasm he had ever experienced, he grunted loudly, "Ah! Ah! Ah!" before he even knew he was making a sound. His head spinning, losing his mind, Zach struggled for air like he'd been submerged under water. When he came around, he sat up with a jolt gaping in complete awe at the handsome man who smiled wickedly at him. "Holy-fucking-shit! Brandon Michael Townsend! Where the hell did you learn to give head like that?"

"Good one?" Brandon asked casually.

"Holy, mother-fucking god..." Zach tried to get his body back under control but still felt his cock throbbing.

"See what you were missing?"

"Brandy...oh, Brandy..." Zach reached out for him. When Zach could get his hands on him he brought Brandon up to his chest and kissed him, sucking at Brandon's soft mouth, licking his jaw, his neck, his earlobe. "I want you to be mine again. Mine, do you hear me?"

"Oh? You moving to New York?" Brandon asked skeptically.

"Yes!"

Sitting up, Brandon looked at him in surprise. "What did you say?"

Still trying to catch his breath, Zach shouted, "Yes! I'm moving to New York! I want to be with you! It's where I need to be."

While Brandon stared at him in awe, Zach knelt up on the bed, shoved Brandon back against the mattress and crawled between Brandon's legs. "I may not have the experience you do, Brandy, but I have the damn desire to please."

"Go for it!" Brandon laughed, his brown eyes sparkling.

Needing no other encouragement, Zach, for the first time in his life, had a man's cock into his mouth. *Oh, no this isn't just any man, this is my Brandy...my beautiful boy next door.* Gripping the base of Brandon's cock like a baseball bat, Zach sucked on it and moved his hands in time with his mouth. Opening his eyes, checking to make sure he was doing it right, Zach found Brandon had closed his and instinctively spread his legs wide. Just remembering, Zach moved his left hand to Brandon's hot heavy balls. Toying with them, trying to keep his rhythm constant, multitasking, Zach tasted the salty drop and bet himself he could swallow. Just as Brandon opened his lips to moan, communicating to Zach the moment was approaching, Zach pushed the tip of his finger up Brandon's ass, just as he had done ten years ago. The charge of electricity flowed like a bolt of lightning. Brandon's come hit the back of Zach's tongue and down it went like an oyster off a shell. Sitting up, licking the tip gently, Zach smiled at Brandon as he recuperated.

"First time sucking a dick?" Brandon panted.

"Yup." It was Zach's turn to sit up and beam proudly.

"Nice job, rookie."

"Thanks, Brandy."

"Now get over here and cuddle. I'm so exhausted I'm going to sleep."

The Boy Next Door

Zach crawled up next to him and wrapped around him. Humming happily in his ear, Zach lavished in the feel of Brandon's sweaty skin and his delicious scent.

"We need a wake up call," Brandon moaned tiredly.

"I just got mine, Brandy. I just got mine," Zach teased happily.

Chapter Sixteen

Zach sat at his desk, reviewing his outstanding cases and trying to determine how long it would take for him to wrap them up and give his notice. Writing up a letter of resignation on the laptop in front of him, he looked up quickly when Jillian entered the office without knocking.

"Where the hell were you all last night?" she accused.

"Out. I told you I was with a friend." He lowered the screen on his computer so she couldn't read it.

"You scumbag. You went back to that freak of a wife!"

"Give me a break, Jillian. We never had anything real between us. It was just an affair."

"Are you ending it?" she gasped, crossing her arms over her chest.

"Yes. So? You going to sue for harassment now? Isn't that the way chicks like you are? You get dumped and you demand money?"

"You son of a bitch!" she spat. "What the hell do you think I am? Some piece of trash you can just toss away?"

About to confirm her suspicions, he added as a preface, "Don't pretend I'm your first conquest in this firm. I know you slept with two other junior associates. So, please, Jillian, don't play the coy little girl."

"Who told you I slept with them?"

"You think gossip doesn't get around in this office?" he laughed.

"If you knew, why did you go out with me?"

"Duh." He tilted his head in an obvious gesture, then replied, "Anything else you need?"

"Find a new legal secretary, asshole!"

As she stormed out, he shouted, "Good timing!" Opening his laptop, he continued writing his resignation letter.

Brandon left the office of opposing, prosecuting council, his pad filled with useless notes. Checking his watch, he flagged down a taxicab and rode back to the hotel, intending on getting the scribbles translated into paragraphs before he forgot what he had written and heard. Tipping the driver generously, Brandon felt light as a feather as he made his way to the hotel lobby. Nodding at the clerk behind the desk, he was about to head to the elevator when the man shouted his name.

"Mr. Townsend!"

"Yes?" Brandon trotted over to him.

"An urgent message."

Slightly concerned, Brandon nodded, took the folded paper with him and opened it as he stood in front of the elevators. As he stepped inside the elevator, he tried his phone, found it couldn't get a signal, and had to be patient until he entered his room. Opening his door, moving across the carpet to the window, Brandon called Lori. "Hey. What's so urgent?"

"Your mom called here. I gave her the hotel number, but I just wanted to call you to make sure you knew she called."

Thinking of Zach's dad, Brandon asked, "Did she say what was wrong?"

"Something about Reece's wife? Is that your sister-in-law?"

"Yes. Did she say what?"

"No. She did indicate she wanted you to call there though. I hope everything is all right. I always think the worst."

"Yeah, well, it usually is the worst." He sat down on the bed and loosened his tie.

"How did today go? Did you get more information?"

"Lori, it's a complete waste of time. I have no idea why Shelby had me come out here. I could have gotten the 'no comment on that issue' over the damn phone."

"Yeah, but at least you got to see that old flame again. What's his name?"

Smiling, Brandon replied, "Zach."

"Mmm. Sounds like a big tough quarterback."

"Exactly. Good call."

"They don't call me Ms. Smarty-pants for nothing."

Brandon chuckled softly.

"You have more interviews lined up for later in the week, right? Ah, wasn't it the deputy head prosecutor? And some witnesses?"

"Yes. But it's pathetic, Lori. No one really is at liberty to discuss the case while the trial is pending. I'm telling you, Shelby is not going to be happy with my vague summary."

"Hey, you got an insider there, Mr. Hunk-Zach. Use him."

"I can't. That would be nasty." Brandon checked his watch.

"So? We've done nasty things before. At least I have."

"No. I won't do that to Zach."

"Oh, well, it was just a thought."

"Let me call my mother. Thanks for calling and leaving a message for me."

"No problem. I hope it's nothing serious."

"Thanks. See ya." Brandon hung up, dialing his old home telephone number in New Jersey where his parents still dwelled.

Picturing his house as the phone rang, Brandon remembered all the good old days. "Mom?"

"Brandon, did you get my message?"

"I just got it now from Lori. Did you try to call the hotel?"

"I did, but I think I got the wrong number."

"What's wrong with Grace? Lori said it had something to do with her?"

After a deep breath, Lois said, "It's not good news, Brandon."

"What?" Brandon kicked off his shoes and moved back on the mattress to lean against the headboard of the bed. From there he noticed he could see his reflection in the mirror on the dresser.

"They found a lump in her breast and she's having a biopsy."

"Oh, shit. How's Reece holding up?"

"Not well. You know your brother. He's always imagining the worst."

"Not to change the subject, Mom, but, did you know Sly Sherman died?" Silence followed. "Mom? You still there?"

"Yes."

"Oh. I didn't hear anything, so I thought maybe my phone had cut out."

"How do you know?"

Suddenly realizing he had to explain his source, Brandon shrugged his shoulders at his reflection as if asking himself if it made any difference. "Uh, well, the funny thing is, I was at a law firm conducting an interview, and who do you think I ran into?"

"Not Zachary."

"Yeah! You believe it?" Brandon chuckled trying to make it all sound light and fluffy.

"Oh, Brandon. How are you? Are you all right?"

Knowing how smart and perceptive his mother was, his façade dropped quickly. "I'm okay. We actually got together and talked for hours about everything."

"Did he tell you why he never contacted you? Why he left you so heartbroken?"

"Yes, Mom, he did." Not wanting to dredge up the degree of pain Zach had suffered, Brandon just said, "It's okay, Mom. I forgive him."

"How did Sly die? Heart attack?"

"No. He fell asleep at the wheel one night."

"Oh, no. Oh, that's terrible. I wish I could call Maude and tell her how sorry I am. When did this happen?"

"I think he said a couple of years ago. Do you want me to get his mom's number?"

"I don't know. It's been so long, Brandon. I got the feeling they all hated us."

"Maybe not. I'll get the number for you, just in case you feel the urge."

"Okay, Brandon. If you want to. When will you be back in New York?"

"I'm scheduled to be back this Friday. You want me sooner?"

"No. No, I don't know what good it will do until we have the results of the tests. Poor thing. She has three young children, Brandon."

"I know, Mom. But it may not be cancer. Don't think the worst." The phone on the desk near the bed rang. Brandon looked at it, saying, "Mom? I'm on my mobile phone and the phone in the room is ringing. You mind if I get it?"

"No. Go ahead."

Brandon cupped his tiny cell phone, picking up the receiver on the nightstand. "Hello?"

"Brandy?"

"Hi, Zach. I've got my mom on my cell phone. Can you hold on a sec?"

"Yeah! No prob."

"Oh, what's your mother's number. Just in case my mom wants to call her, you know, just to say sorry about your dad."

"Oh. Ah…" Zach rattled it off.

"Hang on." Brandon put his mobile phone on his ear, "Mom?"

"Yes, dear?"

"It's Zach on the phone. He told me Maude's number. You got a pen?" Brandon repeated it before it left his short term memory.

"Zach is calling you at your hotel?" Lois asked in surprise. "Are you two…?"

"I don't know." Brandon smiled. "But if we get back together, you'll be the first to know."

"Be careful, Brandon. Don't trust him."

"It's okay, Mom." Brandon said goodbye, then held the other phone to his ear. "Sorry. I'm here."

"Everything okay?"

"Well, Reece's wife may have a health problem. But it's too early to panic."

"I wrote up my resignation letter."

"You what?" Brandon gasped. "Already?"

"Yeah, what the fuck am I waiting for?"

Brandon's eyes found his own in the mirror. "Uh? Time to digest all this?"

"Don't tell me you're changing your mind, Brandy."

"No! Are you insane?"

"Good. Jesus, give me a heart attack."

"When are you going to hand it in?"

"I don't know. They only need two weeks."

"Oh, hey, can you do me a sneaky favor before you quit?"

"What's that?"

Brandon twirled the phone cord around his fingers for a few seconds, then asked, "Uh, you know the story I came here to cover? That big trial and scandal that's been hitting all the papers, the one your firm is defending?"

"You bad boy! You bad, bad boy!"

Smiling, Brandon said, "Hell, at least you're laughing instead of swearing at me for using you."

"I'd get arrested, Brandy."

"I know. Forget it. So, when are you coming by tonight?"

"Now?"

"Good."

"Uh, I bought rubbers…"

"Okay…" Brandon nodded, not getting offended.

"And baby oil."

"Yes! Yes!" Brandon shouted, pumping his fist into the air.

"Great! On my way!"

"Can't wait."

"Bye!"

Brandon hung up, then jumped out of bed to hop in the shower and shave.

Smiling, Zach shut down his computer and put some files away in a metal cabinet. Just as he was getting his jacket on, leaving, he passed by some desks and offices, then paused. There, on Mr. Cade's secretary's desk was *the* file. The one that Brandon had asked for. Zach knew he'd be screwed if he took it. Looking over his shoulder first, he opened it up and read the first page. It was a table of contents. Knowing which witness had given the most damaging testimony, Zach flipped to that page. Another peek around the emptying office and he folded the paper and stuffed into his jacket pocket. He closed the file, leaving, not looking back, trying not to feel nervous. What did he owe these people? He was leaving. Nothing.

Clean, shaved, dabbed with cologne, Brandon straightened the suite quickly, then called room service and had them deliver some wine. The scene set, Brandon stared out the large window at the head and taillights of the traffic below. Somewhere down there was his baby. His soul-mate. The prospect of Zach moving to New York had his head spinning. It must be true love. He hadn't been fooling himself for the last ten years of his life.

When a tiny rap on the door sounded, Brandon felt his heart pumping in excitement. Rushing towards it, he flung it open and found that fantastic man. "Hi," Brandon said shyly, as if it were a first date.

"Hey, Brandy." Zach stepped in, setting a brown paper bag down on the dresser, removing his coat. Once Zach had shed a few layers and was in just his cream-colored cotton long-sleeve shirt and gray work slacks, he scanned the room, spotting the bottle of wine. "Mind if I have a glass?"

"No. Help yourself." Brandon gestured to the table it was set on. As Zach popped the cork and tipped two glasses full, Brandon had a peek into the brown paper bag. "My, weren't you brave." He held up a tube of lubrication.

Looking back over his shoulder, Zach shrugged then raised one of the glasses to his lips.

Brandon set the three items from the bag onto the nightstand; condoms, lubrication, and the infamous baby oil.

"You hungry?" Brandon asked as an air of awkwardness clouded the room. What were they supposed to do? Just strip and hop in the sack? Where were they in this relationship?

"No." Zach set the wine glass down after nearly emptying

it down his throat.

For a moment they both stood still, staring at each other. To end the strange silence, Brandon asked, "Am I supposed to ask you how your day was?" In a high voice, he teased, "Honey? Did you have a good day at the office?"

Zach smiled.

Moving to sit on the bed near him, Brandon tilted his head and whispered, "Are you okay?"

"Yeah." Zach puffed up in defense at the concern, but it soon deflated. Dropping down next to Brandon, he lowered his eyes and muttered, "Just trying to gauge in my head how soon I can move."

"Oh?" Brandon caressed Zach's broad back.

"Yeah. Uh, this damn divorce…"

"You said you were in negotiations. What exactly is going on?"

After a very loud exhale that sounded like frustration to Brandon, Zach replied, "Brook is fighting me on everything. I swear, Brandy, until she completely bankrupts me, she won't let it go."

"What is she entitled to, you know, legally?"

"That's where the debate begins." Zach straightened his back and then slumped over again. "She wants the house, alimony, half my retirement accounts…blah, blah, blah…and the fucked up part is she's worth what I'm worth. She's been working the same length of time, has the same income, the same IRAs. She should be happy with fifty percent."

The last thing Brandon wanted to do was discuss Zach's failed marriage. It wasn't exactly foreplay. "What's the deal, then? If she's worth the same, why won't the judges just give her half?"

"Because…" Zach cringed, mumbling, "I cheated on her."

"So? Oh, come on, Zach. That's not even rare anymore."

"Yeah, but it shows who's to blame for the failure of the marriage. Most judges have it in their heads to punish the wrong-doer."

Brandon stood up abruptly, turning his back to Zach. What was he thinking? Why did he want to get involved with this man? He wasn't the same person. The baggage was already suffocating.

"I'm sorry, Brandon. I'll shut up now."

Rubbing his forehead, Brandon tried to think if this was worth the trouble. Before he made that decision, he felt a hand rest on his shoulder. Turning around to face Zach, Brandon once again fell into the grip of those powerfully hypnotic blue irises.

"I'm sorry, Brandon. It's my problem. I shouldn't burden you with it. I suppose I just need to vent sometimes."

"I understand." Brandon knew they only had two more days until he flew back to New York. Sadly, he wondered if once he was out of sight, would he be out of mind as well.

Zach clasped Brandon's hand and drew him back to sit on the bed. Once they were side by side, Zach whispered, "Remember what we did with that baby oil, Brandy?"

Chuckling to himself, Brandon did.

"Wanna do it again?"

A big grin spread across Brandon's mouth at the memory.

Zach began to undress, his eyes never leaving Brandon's.

Wanting Zach to take the lead as he had done ten years ago, Brandon watched the material drop from Zach's body until he was naked. Keeping his eye on him, Brandon followed Zach's progress to that nightstand and the small bottle of clear liquid. Zach uncapped it, pouring some into his cupped palm. Once he set the bottle down, he rubbed his hands together, then proceeded to coat his chest and tight abdomen with glistening oil.

Brandon watched, enthralled.

Going back to the bottle again and again until he was completely coated, Zach stood tall. Turning his palms to face forward, he beckoned for Brandon to come to him.

The sight of that slick, glistening torso had Brandon in heat. Salivating at the curves of Zach's pectoral muscles, the way the light gleamed off their domed mounds, his egg-carton abdomen and his slippery thighs, Brandon stood up slowly and began undressing, his sight never moving from that ultimate specimen of masculinity.

Once he was naked, Brandon crossed the room to Zach's outstretched hands. And just like he had done in that hotel room back in Kissimmee, Brandon embraced Zach, then they squirmed against each other, slipping and sliding across taut flesh, moaning in anticipation of things to come.

Rubbing his body all over Zach's, Brandon closed his eyes and arched his back so just his pelvis was connected to Zach's. Loving the slick surface and rough pubic hair, Brandon felt light-headed from his body's demand for satisfaction.

Through his clouded senses, Brandon heard Zach whisper, "Brandy...look at you."

Cracking his eyes open, seeing Zach staring down at him, the connection of their hips, Brandon couldn't stop rubbing against those thighs, that erection.

Someone had to make a move. Zach picked Brandon up in his arms and brought him to the bed. Once Brandon was reclining back on it, Zach tipped more drops of oil onto Brandon's chest.

Panting, looking down at the beading circles of liquid, Brandon couldn't stop his ribs from rising and falling rapidly as his excitement grew. Zach's masculine hand began smoothing the oil all over Brandon's body. When that oily palm gripped Brandon's cock, Brandon clenched his jaw on the intensity of the pleasure surge between his legs. Zach starting jerking Brandon off, the oil making it smooth and slippery. Just before Brandon felt the urge to come, Zach stopped.

Brandon waited as Zach opened a condom, then slid it onto Brandon's cock. Waiting, staring at Zach as if he were the expert in gay sex and not the reverse, Brandon watched as Zach impaled himself on Brandon's erection. Brandon gripped the bedspread under him and held on for dear life. Zach rose up and down on Brandon's hard cock, watching Brandon's face for his reaction.

Choking at the surge to his loins, Brandon came and ground his jaw at the intensity. Zach disengaged their connection, removed the spent condom, rolled a fresh one onto his own cock. Nudging Brandon's legs back, Zach exposed his ass.

Still recuperating from the orgasm, Brandon wrapped his arms around his legs to hold them up for Zach. When Zach penetrated him, Brandon clenched his jaw once more and felt that slick hard cock sliding in and out of him like silk. Hearing Zach's grunts of pleasure, Brandon opened his eyes to watch his face, savoring the orgasmic expression on Zach's fantastic features.

Slowly pulling out, Zach dropped the second condom on the floor, unfolded Brandon's legs and crawled to rest on top of him.

Feeling Zach's weight, adoring him, Brandon wrapped his arms around Zach's broad back and fell fast asleep.

Chapter Seventeen

The next morning, after an automated wake up call, Brandon roused Zach from a deep slumber and they tumbled around the sheets for a quick morning screw. Once showered and dressed, Brandon checked the time and was about to ask Zach what his plans were for the night, when Zach produced a piece of paper from out of his suit jacket pocket.

"What's this?" Brandon looked down at it skeptically.

"Take a look." Zach gave it to him, continuing to knot his tie in the mirror.

Unfolding it, realizing what it was, Brandon choked and said, "What did you do? I can't believe this!"

"Will that help you with your article?"

"Yes, but how can I use it? I mean, they'll want to know where the leak came from."

Zach shrugged, then stood back to check out his reflection in the mirror.

"Zach, I can't risk it." Brandon wanted the information, very badly. "Look, there'll be an investigation and no doubt someone will figure it out." He handed Zach back the paper.

Moving past the page Brandon was holding out to him, Zach picked up his coat and replied, "You decide what you want to do. I don't care, Brandy."

"How can you not care? Zachary..."

"Because I owe you for what happened between us. And you mean more to me than anyone in that office. So, it's yours to do with as you like. I have to go. What time do you want me here?"

Brandon tossed the paper on the bed, moving closer to Zach on the pretext of straightening his tie. "Where do you live? Should we meet at your house?" Brandon didn't expect the reaction he got. Zach lowered his head and his mouth formed a bitter line. Stepping back, Brandon exclaimed, "Oh, right. You still live with your wife, don't you?"

"Wait…Brandon, don't get all bent out of shape…"

"Why didn't you say something? Why didn't you tell me you two still cohabitated?" Brandon felt crushed.

"Because it's meaningless. She's intending on taking the house from me. I told you that. Did you think she would get it if she moved out?"

"Where does she think you are when you don't come home?" Brandon put his hands on his hips defensively. "With the blonde bimbo?"

Zach threw down his coat and confronted Brandon. "Why are you doing this? We had a fantastic night. Why are you ruining it?"

Brandon threw up his hands in exasperation. "Me? I'm not the one with a wife at home and a pussy on the side!"

As if he couldn't leave until this was resolved, Zach sat down on the bed and dragged Brandon with him. "Brandy, calm down."

"You know how many times you have said that since last Monday?"

"I have to. You overreact."

Brandon was about to explode.

And Zach seemed to know it. He gripped Brandon by the jaw and turned his stubborn face to meet his. "I'm divorcing her. I'm quitting my job. I'm moving back to New York.

Hello?"

Still Brandon was seething. "Oh, that sounds so simple! So easy to accomplish."

"No. It's not easy, Brandon, but it's certainly not impossible. Just let me do it."

"How long? Huh? How long will it be this time? Ten years?"

"Brandon!"

At the furious tone, Brandon bit his lip. It was Sly's voice. Sly's angry shout coming out of Zach. Wanting to tear out of Zach's gripping hand, Brandon fought with his anger to push him away.

And that hand held on to his jaw like a clamp. "Brandy…I'm not going to tell you to calm down again because it'll aggravate you, but…" Zach inhaled a deep breath and continued, "give me some time. Okay? Yes, I fucked up my life. I know that. But it's not some permanent disaster that we can't deal with. No. It won't be ten fucking years."

Breaking down, feeling seventeen, Brandon whimpered, "But, I want you now. I don't want to go back to New York without you."

A warm smile found Zach's lips. "Oh, Christ, you are so adorable."

Brandon closed his eyes as Zach's mouth connected to his. Wrapping around his neck, Brandon sucked at his tongue, his lips, tears running down his cheeks.

They fell back on the bed with a bounce and kissed passionately for a few minutes. Zach broke the spell and checked his watch. "I have to go, Brandy."

Nodding, wiping at his eyes, Brandon said, "Okay."

Standing up, walking with Zach to the door, Brandon whispered, "You'll come by after work?"

"You know I will."

"Good. Ah, meet me in the lounge? Have a drink first?"

"Yes. Keep your mobile phone on so I can tell you I'm on my way."

"Okay," Brandon replied, nodding.

"See ya later, Brandy."

Zach pecked him on the lips, then left. When he did, Brandon felt a hole in his heart at Zach's departure, and knew it would be hell on Friday when he boarded his plane.

His final interview conducted, the summary of his report lacking terribly for a good read in the magazine, Brandon had a moral dilemma on his hands. Standing outside the county courthouse, he leaned against the building, away from the biting wind and dialed his mobile phone. "Lori? Can you talk?"

"Yeah, babe, what's up?"

"Well, I interviewed the prosecutor and his staff."

"And?"

"Got nothing." Brandon bit his lip.

"You have to be kidding me?"

"No. I can't believe this."

"No one will say anything of value?"

"No." Brandon watched some pedestrians walk by, hunched over against the stiff breeze. "But…"

"But?"

"Zachary came through with a tidbit."

"Oh!" Lori giggled. "Juicy bits?"

"Very juicy."

"There you go! An exclusive. You'll make Shelby come in his pants."

Cringing at that image, Brandon replied, "Ew, thanks for a nauseating mental picture."

"Sorry. So? What's the problem? Get typing."

"Lori, what if Zachary gets caught. He could go to jail."

"Isn't he a lawyer?"

"Yes."

"Well, he knows better than most what he's risking. Obviously, you're worth that risk."

Brandon looked around the streets as cars, taxis, and trucks rumbled past him.

"Hello? You still there?"

"Yeah." Brandon sighed. "I can't. I can't risk it."

"Wow. This guy means a lot to you, doesn't he?"

"More than I want to admit. The S.O.B."

"Okay. Just write the fluff. It's not your fault no one was giving out anything good."

"Yes. Right. I'll do that."

"See ya tomorrow? You coming into the office after your flight?"

"Yes. I will for a few hours. It comes in at around noon."

"Good. See you then. Have a safe trip."

"Thanks." He hung up and then waved down a taxi to take him back to the hotel.

"Yes, I know." Brandon nodded his head, his cell phone to his ear, seated at the desk in his room, the laptop open and his article half written. "Mom, at least it's not cancer. So, it's a lump. Let them take it out and she'll be fine."

"Yes. You're right, Brandon. It is good news."

"I assume Reece is relieved."

"Of course. He just wants it to be over and done with."

"When is the surgery?"

"I don't know. When will you be home, Brandon?"

"Tomorrow, around noon."

"Can you come by over the weekend for dinner?"

"Sure." He checked his watch for the time.

"I phoned Maude."

"Did you?" That amused Brandon.

"She seemed happy to hear from me."

"Good."

"I didn't tell her about you and Zach. I said I just looked her up. I know she'd be upset if I mentioned it."

"Yes. I think she'd be upset as well." Brandon frowned despite himself. "Look, Mom, let me go. I have to get this article finished and sent to Shelby."

"Okay, Brandon. Call me when you're back at your place."

"I will." He hung up and set the mobile phone on the desk next to him. Peering at the paper that lay folded beside it, Brandon bit his lip and opened it, reading the damning testimony. It was so deliciously good, so intriguing, he wanted to use it. Shelby would be amazed he had gotten that much information, more than any other journalist had to date, pre-trial. "Oh, Zachary, why always the moral dilemma from you, huh?"

Brandon set the paper down and continued typing, his fingers flying over the keyboard.

Zach left the courthouse and stood outside the building, trying to withstand the biting wind. He dialed Brandon's mobile phone, walking to where he had parked his car.

"Hello?"

"Finally! Brandon, I've been trying to get through to you."

"Oh. Here I am. You on your way?"

"Yes, I'm on my way."

"I'll be waiting."

Zach disconnected the call and continued walking to the

parking garage. When the cell phone rang again, he sighed tiredly and said hello.

"I assume you're not coming home again tonight."

"What difference does it make, Brook? You want the fucking house, you got the fucking house."

"Are you sleeping at that whore's place every night?"

"Like I said, what difference would it make?" He used his key fob to open the lock to his car door.

"I swear, Zach, I'll make your life miserable."

"You already have, Brook." He sat down in the driver's seat and closed the door. "Look, I've changed my mind. You want everything? Take it. I'm not fighting in court over it."

"What? Why? What's going on? You said you wouldn't give up over my dead body."

"Life's too short, Brook. I can't stand the idea of seeing you in court every day, or paying some stupid divorce lawyer tens of thousands of dollars. What do you want? Name it?"

"What the hell are you up to? I don't trust you, you dirty slimeball."

"I need a fresh start. I want to quit my job and get the hell out of here." He stuck his key in the ignition but didn't start the engine.

"Quit? Oh, great, now you won't be able to afford alimony."

"I'll get another job."

"Where? Where are you going? Are you moving in with that slut?"

Rubbing his face, he repeated, "Why the hell do you care?"

"Because," she screeched, "I don't want her to have you!"

"I'm not going anywhere with Jillian. I broke it off with her."

"You did?"

"Yes." He started the car and shut off the radio

"Good. She's nasty, Zachary. I hate her."

"Look, just tell me what I have to do to get out of this marriage, will ya? I need to get on with my life, Brook. I can't keep living like this, in limbo."

"Why? So you can find some other bimbo to screw?" she sneered.

Sick of the lies, thinking about all the times he had spent in counseling with his therapist urging him to accept himself as who he was, Zach blurted out, "No. I don't want to be with a woman because I'm in love with a man."

The stunned silence that followed caused him to believe she hung up. "Brook?"

"You moron. You really try everything to get me to feel sorry for you and make this divorce easy."

Exhaling in frustration, Zach replied, "Yeah, whatever. You believe what you want."

"You? Gay? You must be joking. You know how many women you've fucked?"

"Too many." Zach checked his watch.

"Suddenly, the big macho man says he's gay. That's unbelievable, Zach. Nice try."

"Whatever. I have to go. I'll call my lawyer and tell him to agree to your terms."

"Go? Wait a minute...does this mean you're staying over at some guy's house now? Is that what's going on? You've shacked up with a homosexual?"

"Sort of. Not exactly. But that's close enough. He's waiting. See ya." He hung up before her rebuttal. The phone rang immediately and he shut it off. Backing out of the parking space, he smiled. "Damn, that felt good!"

Brandon nervously paced the length of the hotel room. He

had already begun to pack his clothing in anticipation of the early check-out and ride to the airport the next morning. Finally, he heard that familiar knock on the door. Racing to open it, Brandon grabbed Zach's arm and dragged him inside his room, leaping on him, embracing him, kissing him passionately.

Zach reacted in surprise, wrapping his arms around Brandon in response.

Once Brandon felt he had a good long kissing session, he stepped back and smiled with a silly grin. "Hello. Come in. Take off your coat."

"Wow. Miss me?" Zach dropped his coat and his suit jacket on the chair.

"Yes. Come here. I finished the article. It's on the screen if you're interested in reading it." Brandon pointed to the laptop on the desk.

"Not really, but I should see if you're as talented as you were at writing back in high school." Zach sat down on the chair in front of it as Brandon stood behind him, massaging his neck and shoulders as he read.

Rereading it, Brandon wondered what Zach would think of his writing skills.

After he finished, Zach spun around in his chair and smiled at Brandon. "Amazing. I'll tell ya, Brandy, you are very talented. You did a great job covering the tracks, babe."

"Mmm, talented in many ways." Brandon sat on Zach's lap, purring.

"You're leaving in the morning, aren't you?"

"Yes. The flight is for nine. I thought I told you that."
"You told me you were leaving Friday. I didn't know the time."

Brandon cuddled Zach as he rested his head on Brandon's chest. Brandon kissed Zach's hair and caressed it gently, running his fingers through it. "I know. I can't believe we're going to be pulled apart again."

"Not for long."

The Boy Next Door

Brandon felt Zach nudge him, so he stood off his lap. Zach began opening the buttons of his dress shirt. "This time it's temporary, Brandy."

"It better be. My heart can't take it again, Zach. I swear I'll crack up."

"As long as it takes to give notice, sign the divorce papers, and book a flight."

"That fast?" Brandon laughed at the joke as Zach undressed.

"That fast."

"I thought you anticipated a long extended court battle."

Tossing the last article of his clothing on the chair, Zach replied, "Nope. I'm giving her everything."

"What? Don't do that! Are you nuts?"

Zach jumped on the bed, propping up his jaw in his palm. "No. I'm finally not nuts. I know what I've been missing, and where I need to be."

"Zachary, don't give her more than she deserves. You'll regret it and hate me."

"Why are you still dressed?"

Brandon started taking off his shirt. "Zach, I'm not kidding. Even if it takes a little longer, don't give up all your assets."

"Brandy, I don't give a shit about it. I used to. I used to think that was what was important. A big fucking house, a Jag, the bank account...it's crap. Useless crap."

Dropping his briefs, Brandon climbed over the bed to mirror Zach's position. "Crap? All of it? So, now you're throwing away all your worldly possessions?"

"Come on, Brandy. I'll get another job in Manhattan and build up the assets again. But seriously, you want me to spend thousands of dollars, waste months of our time, fighting that bitch in court?"

Considering that option, Brandon answered, "Hell no."

"Good. Get over here."

Brandon allowed Zach to maneuver him so he was on top of Zach's body. Spreading his legs, Brandon straddled Zach's hips, leaning up on his elbows to smile down at him. "How long do you think it'll take?"

"Baby, I'll be home for Christmas," Zach laughed teasingly.

Blinking in surprise, Brandon asked, "Two months?"

"Yeah. What have I got to pack? I'll just sell the car, take my clothes, and fly over."

When Zach's face darkened a moment, Brandon tilted his head curiously and asked, "What's wrong?"

"I never thought to ask. Ah, am I moving in with you, or do you want me to get my own place?"

Brandon hit Zach's shoulder playfully. "Get your own place? You dork!"

"Okay. I just never got the invite to move in, formally."

Wiggling his hips first, Brandon then announced, "I formally invite you, Zachary Emerson Sherman, to come and live with me, Brandon Michael Townsend, in my luxury condo in New York City."

"Luxury condo? Woo woo! I accept, Mr. Townsend."

"Good. Now let's get down to business. It's our last night until Christmas."

Zach urged Brandon down to his mouth, kissing him hotly.

Moaning at the fire, Brandon couldn't wait.

Chapter Eighteen

His suitcase packed, his laptop tucked away in its case, Brandon stood at the doorway, ready to check out.

"I'm driving you," Zach insisted

"You'll be late for work."

"Fuck work." Zach gestured to the door.

Standing with Brandon as he checked out at the desk, returning the room key and signing the credit card slip, Zach waited patiently. Together they walked to the parking garage just as a light snowfall began to shimmer from the cloudy sky.

"Too bad it's not a blizzard. I'd stay another day." Brandon stared up at the dizzying flakes.

Smiling sadly at the missed opportunity, Zach used his key fob to unlock the doors of his car.

"Oh, you really do have a Jaguar," Brandon said as he climbed in.

"Big deal. I used to think it was a status symbol. Now I know it's just another liability I can't wait to get rid of." He started the engine and began their drive to the airport.

"My, haven't we grown up, Zachary," Brandon mused, reaching to hold Zach's hand.

"I suppose so. Some times I don't feel twenty-seven. I feel sixteen and stupid."

"Join the club. I wonder when maturity kicks in?" Brandon smiled at him.

"Never in my case." Zach smiled back, squeezing Brandon's hand.

As they drew nearer to the airport exit and departure terminal, Zach's mood began to sink. He didn't want Brandon to go, not even if it meant only a few months of separation. Even one day was too long.

"Just drop me off—" Brandon started to say.

"Fuck that. I'm parking and going in with you."

"They won't let you go to the gate."

"They will if I buy a ticket."

"Zach, don't waste your money."

"Shut up." Zach parked, slipping the parking voucher into his wallet, reaching to help Brandon carry his suitcase. Before Brandon could stop him, Zach was in line at the ticketing booth, buying a ticket to New York so he could get past security. Brandon checked his bag and they went through the metal detectors and into the main terminal area.

"We have an hour. How about a drink?" Zach pointed to a lounge near the gate.

"Sure."

Even though Brandon smiled, Zach knew he was struggling with the separation as well. It brought back very painful memories. Sitting together on high stools at a miniature round table that faced the tarmac and the assortment of jumbo jets, they sipped a ridiculously expensive beer, which cost triple what it would outside the airport, and sat in silence. Zach knew if he talked about anything, he would get emotional. It was hard enough sitting there knowing the clock was ticking.

While they drank more beer and exchanged light chit-chat, the moment they dreaded was drawing near. An announcement for boarding sounded over the PA system.

Brandon stood off the stool, his head drooping. "Well...this is it."

Zach followed him to the desk where the attendants were checking boarding passes.

"You have my home number and address," Brandon confirmed. "I'll call you when I arrive just so you know I'm there. I'll most likely go to Mom's over the weekend for dinner and to see Reece and Grace."

Nodding, numb, Zach was listening but trying not to at the same time. He hated this goodbye. Seeing Brandon wrapping up his conversation, about to make a move to leave, Zach did what he never thought he would ever do in his life.

When Zach grabbed Brandon into an embrace and went for his lips, Brandon's eyes sprang open in shock. In the middle of boarding among hundreds of people, Zachary Sherman outed himself. Brandon closed his eyes and wrapped his arms around Zach's broad back, ignoring the passing gasps or whispers of disapproval. That hot mouth was letting Brandon know just how missed, how loved, and how needed he was. And Brandon didn't care who else knew it.

When the time grew too close, Zach parted from Brandon's mouth softly.

Brandon found the two running rivers of tears down Zachary's face. "Don't cry." Brandon wiped at Zach's cheeks, holding back his own tidal wave.

"I love you," Zach mouthed silently, gripped to Brandon's hands.

"I love you too, babe..." Brandon tried to smile but when he did, tears cascaded down his face.

"Call me," Zach squeaked out of his closing throat.

Nodding, unable to speak, Brandon wiped at his eyes and handed his boarding pass to the attendant. She smiled sweetly at him.

Through the ropes and headed down the aisle to the airplane, Brandon kept looking back to see Zach's devastated face. He knew why it was so painful, he knew.

When Brandon looked back for the last time, then vanished, Zach almost broke down. Hurrying out of the terminal, avoiding anyone who stared, he found his way back to his car and sat down behind the steering wheel. Alone in the confines of his car, he broke down and sobbed, just like he had the last time he had been separated from Brandon. Resigned to get out to New York ASAP, Zach pulled himself together and headed to work to put in his resignation letter.

Chapter Nineteen

The Christmas tree sparkled with multicolored lights and baubles. A light snow had coated the lawns and trees in Fair Lawn. The Townsend family gathered around the glowing tree as the grandchildren squealed in delight and opened their gifts.

Brandon stood at the threshold, watching the action. Grace was sitting on Reece's lap, her recovery almost complete from minor surgery. Brandon's mother and dad looked happy, rosy and content to have the whole family together.

Trying to feel a part of them and not an outsider, Brandon smiled, nodding his head as his nieces waved their new toys to show him.

Two months, hundreds of emails and phone calls later, Brandon felt no closer to getting Zach into his life than he did ten years ago. No, he reminded himself, this was different. They spoke every day, had phone sex every night. No, this wasn't the way they had left it ten years ago.

But Brandon thought there was a promise. A promise to be with him by Christmas. *Well? It's December twenty-fifth. Where are you?*

During the last phone call Zach had relayed some delay in signing the divorce papers. Some added complication, some technicality. Whatever you called it, it was a delay.

"Uncle Brandon! Look!"

Brandon smiled. "Very nice!" He caught his mother's sad, knowing smile. She knew. She knew who he was missing. What did Santa bring him this year? Another Christmas on his own? Another New Year's Eve going to bed at ten o'clock?

Lois whispered to Mel, "We should tell him about Zach's phone call, dear."

"No. Zach wanted to surprise him, Lois."

"But it's just the weather delaying the flight. Look at him, Mel. He looks so sad."

"But think of the look on his face when Zachary walks through that door."

Nodding reluctantly in agreement, Lois' attention was brought back to her grandchildren.

Needing to move away from the noise, Brandon climbed the familiar stairs to his old room. It was much the same as it had been when he lived there. Walking to his window, he could see the corner of the swimming pool next door, a blue cover on it, frosted in snow. He didn't know the neighbors now. He didn't care to.

Pausing, staring at his bed wistfully, he never had Zach in it. Never made love to him on that bed. But there, on the carpet, Zach used to reach down the front of Brandon's pants. As they studied, as Brandon read, caught them up on their assignments, Zach's warm hand would knead his crotch, fondling his soft cock, groping his balls.

"Ah, the good ol' days," Brandon whispered, laughing to himself. "Where are you Zach? Change your mind? Have second thoughts about being a gay man in Manhattan?"

The noise of excitement downstairs grew louder. Brandon wondered what new gadget his brother bought for his nieces now. How much crap did the kids need? Well, their mother had a health scare. That was probably why.

About to give up on his reminiscing, Brandon turned to the hallway and the landing at the top of the stairs. A man stood there.

It took a moment, but Brandon finally realized who it was. "What the fuck?"

"Hello, Brandy."

"Did you...did you just get here?"

"I did. My flight was delayed in Boston from all the snow. I made your mom promise not to tell you I was on my way." Zach stuffed his gloves into his coat pocket.

"You...I didn't hear the doorbell."

"I rang it. Your mom answered it." Zach laughed.

"She knew?" Brandon felt his skin set on fire. It had only been two months, but what a long two months it had been.

"Swore her to secrecy, sorry. I wanted it to be a surprise." Zach grinned, sliding his wool coat off his broad shoulders.

"I...you said there was some complication. That you couldn't come out..." Seeing that wry grin on Zach's face, Brandon began laughing. "You son of a bitch!"

"Merry Christmas, Brandy."

"You son of a bitch!" Brandon shouted louder, racing across the room and embracing him.

"Mmm, you smell good. A mixture of your mom's home cooking and sex!"

Brandon burst out laughing as a hard cock thrust against his own. "Oh, Zachary Sherman, you are something else."

"Kiss me, you fool." Zach dipped Brandon dramatically.

Brandon grabbed onto him for dear life and connected to his mouth. Kissing him hungrily, Brandon felt dizzy, but content. *Finally!*

After smooching for a long while, Brandon whispered, "We should get back down there. We're being unsociable."

"We do have all night to…" Zach humped Brandon's leg.

"Exactly." Brandon pecked his lips, holding his hand as they descended the stairs to the waiting family. When they came into the living room, everyone stopped talking, staring and smiling at them.

"Mom! You devil! How could you not tell me!" Brandon shouted in a tease. "Guess what Santa Claus brought me!"

His parents exchanged cheeky smiles, then they all gathered around for a hug and a kiss in congratulations.

Standing back to admire him, Brandon couldn't wipe the smile off his face as everyone welcomed Zachary back into the family. When he could, Zach winked at him, giving him a secret smile.

Chapter Twenty

July 2007

"Yes…that's great news. Okay. Yes…" Brandon nodded, hearing the shower running in the master bathroom.

"Are you listening, Brandon? You did it."

"I know. Thanks. I do appreciate it that you called to tell me, Lori. Really."

"Well? Shout or something! Open a bottle of champagne!"

"Yes! I will go out and celebrate!"

"When? Can I come?"

"Yes, you're invited."

"Good. I can get drunk and sit on that hunk again."

"No, you can't sit on Zach's lap again! Silly girl." He laughed. "Let me go. I'll talk to you soon." Brandon hung up, following the sound of Zach singing in the shower.

Standing at the door, staring at Zach's beige outline through the shower doors, Brandon shook his head in awe. "What a bod. What an amazing bod."

"Huh?" Zach opened the shower doors and poked his head out. "You say something, Brandy?"

Approaching him, Brandon admired his wet nakedness and said, "That was Lori on the phone. She just called to tell me my book made it to the New York Times Best Seller list."

"Congratulations! See, she was right. You're better off writing books." Zach shut off the faucets and reached for a towel.

"Yeah. I suppose. Beats going on business trips all the time."

Zach stepped out of the tub, rubbing the towel over his back. "Beats you being gone all the time."

"Exactly." Brandon stared at Zach's muscles as he moved his arms. "Uh, she wants to celebrate."

"Okay."

"Drinks later?"

"Cool."

Brandon nodded, watching as Zach draped the towel over the shower door. Mesmerized by Zach's physique, Brandon began to have carnal thoughts.

As if Zach could read his mind, he reached into the cabinet under the sink and took out a bottle.

To Brandon's delight, Zach began pouring baby oil into his palm, then smoothing it all over his large pectoral muscles.

"Oh, Zachary, I do adore you."

"Come and get it, Brandy."

"You know, there is something to be said about novels that end with H.E.A."

"H.E.A.?" Zach asked, smoothing his oily hand into his pubic hair. "What the hell is that?"

"Happily ever after, lover."

"I thought those were the only types of novels you wrote." Zach set the bottle down and caressed his body with his oily hands, enticing Brandon.

"They are now!" Brandon began to strip off his clothing.

Zach turned his palms forward, invitingly.

Once he was naked, Brandon rushed for that embrace. Sliding his body all over this big muscular hunk, Brandon sighed, "Oh, Zach, I am so glad you're back."

"Brandon, let me tell you something," Zach replied, squeezing Brandon's ass tight, "There's no place like home."

"Oh, that's original." Brandon chuckled.

"Shut up and kiss me."

Brandon connected to his lips and moaned in delight.

The End

About the Author

Award-winning author G. A. Hauser was born in Fair Lawn, New Jersey, USA, and attended university in New York City. She moved to Seattle, Washington where she worked as a patrol officer with the Seattle Polic Department. In early 2000 G.A. moved to Hertfordshire, England, where she began her writing in earnest and published her first book, *In the Shadow of Alexander*. Now a full-time writer in Ohio, G.A. has written dozens of novels, including several bestsellers of gay fiction. For more information on other books by G.A., visit the author at her official website at: www.authorgahauser.com.

G.A. has won awards from All Romance eBooks for Best Novel 2007, *Secrets and Misdemeanors*, Best Author 2007. Best Novel 2008, *Mile High*, and Best Author 2008.

The G.A. Hauser Collection

Available Now
Single Titles

Double Trouble
Pirates
Miller's Tale
Vampire Nights
Teacher's Pet
In the Shadow of Alexander
The Rise and Fall of the Sacred Band of Thebes

The Action Series

Acting Naughty
Playing Dirty
Getting it in the End
Behaving Badly
Dripping Hot

Men in Motion Series

Mile High
Cruising
Driving Hard
Leather Boys

Rescue Series

Man to Man
Two In Two Out
Top Men

G.A. Hauser
Writing as Amanda Winters

Sister Moonshine
Nothing Like Romance
Silent Reign
Butterfly Suicide
Mutley's Crew

Coming Soon
Single Titles

All Man
Heart of Steele
It Takes a Man
Got Men?
In The Dark and What Should Never Be, Erotic Short Stories
Mark and Sharon (formerly titled A Question of Sex)